THE BRACELET

BECKY ARCHIBALD

Printed in the United States of America

ISBN: 978-1-953910-91-2 (hardcover)
ISBN: 978-1-953910-92-9 (paperback)
ISBN: 978-1-953910-93-6 (ebook)

Canoe Tree
Press

4697 Main Street
Manchester Center, VT 05255

Canoe Tree Press is a division of DartFrog Books.

I want to dedicate this book to God. Without his constant help and the determination he gave me to write, this dream wouldn't be possible.

In loving memory of my mom Rose and my dad Bill.

I am thankful to the kind people that helped me bring this book to life. Thank you for making my dream a reality.

To the readers, I hope you enjoy this book.

"Don't change so people like you.
Be yourself and the right people will love the real you."
—Anonymous.

"Always be a first rate version of yourself and not a second rate
version of someone else."
—Judy Garland

"You are a very special person.
There is only one like you in the whole world.
There's never been anyone exactly like you before,
and there will never be again.
Only you.
And people can like you exactly as you are."
—Fred Rogers

"If they don't like you for being yourself,
be yourself even more."
—Taylor Swift.

CHAPTER ONE

I hear a noise...I am startled. The sound isn't the leaves I hear blowing and scraping the ground outside. The sound is coming from my dream. I am so scared. My heart is beating rapidly, and I can feel my palms sweating. I don't understand the meaning of my dream . . . it is so confusing. I want to wake up, but it's like I can't. My eyes feel like they are glued shut, but I know that is impossible. I can feel my eyes twitching, trying to wake myself up, but my curiosity keeps me from interrupting my dream. I just want to understand . . . to learn more, if you know what I mean.

I am in what appears to be a moat in a nearby castle. The moat is deep, really deep, and filled with as much water that could fill a small lake. I am dressed in what looks like a lady servant's uniform of the Medieval era. My dress is pink, of course, which is my favorite color. But that's not what is bothering me . . . it . . . it, I am almost afraid to name it; it is the purple, fire-breathing dragon that is roaring and growling at me and this really cute guy who is standing at my side, who seems to be trying to protect me or shield me from this angry, colorful dragon. The dragon has long, beautiful eyelashes, a little poof of blonde hair at the top of her head, and even red nail polish on its feet. It's crazy; I had never seen a dragon like this, not even when I was little. This dragon seems to know a lot about fashion. A fashionista dragon? That sounds really bizarre, but also quite hilarious.

Anyway, as my dream continues, the whole situation becomes scarier. I could feel the guy, who was wearing a narrow, pointed, blue hat with a red feather sticking out on top, was holding me tightly around my stomach. I felt safe with him, but I had no idea of his identity. All I could see were his bright blue eyes and his blue prince costume.

It was like he knew me, too, but I have never seen him in my life. I wonder who he is. But just as I was trying to figure all of this out, the dragon roared, which felt like an earthquake that almost knocked us down. We didn't fall, but we held each other tighter.

"Cynthia," the blue-eyed prince yelled as the fire came toward us. "Watch out, my love. I will save you." He stepped out in front of me and pointed his sword directly in the dragon's face. The dragon opened her mouth like she was going to eat him, and then that's when I quickly rose up and began to scream and breathe heavily.

My mom Cassandra and my dad Jonathan Adams rushed through my room like a pack of wolves searching for prey.

"Are you okay?" my dad asked with a worried expression on his face.

My mom sat on my bed and placed her hand on my forehead. "She doesn't have a temperature, Jonathan. Did you have a bad dream?"

I couldn't say a word. I was freaking out. All I could do was nod my head up and down. What else could I do? I couldn't explain my dream to my parents; they would think I was weird. Wouldn't they? I mean . . . I dream of the most hottest guy I have ever seen, and he risks his life for me and calls me his love. *How romantic*, I thought, as I pictured little pink hearts floating in the air. Wait! The hearts break apart, pop, and disappear into thin air. How could I feel this way with someone I have never met? It is a little strange, but I felt like I knew him even though we hadn't officially met in real life.

The only thing is that I don't know him, and I just couldn't tell my parents anything . . . not just yet, anyway. They might not believe that I like a guy that I interacted with in a dream.

A smile appeared on my face, and my parents seemed to be more relaxed as they knew I wasn't scared anymore. Well . . . it isn't every day that you dream of a fashionista dragon and a handsome prince who is willing to risk his life for you. I will cherish this moment for the rest of my life.

"I am so glad you are feeling better, honey," my mom said. "I was so afraid that you were sick and was going to miss your first day of high school."

"I can't believe our daughter is already in high school," my dad replied. "Where has all of the time gone?"

My mom and dad both walked to the door and stepped out into the small hallway that led to the stairs. The door shut for about thirty seconds and reopened again. My mom's face appeared in the slightly opened doorway. She smiled at me with her bright white teeth and her face full of makeup. She looked really nice as always . . . I just didn't notice it earlier since I was thinking about my dream prince with those beautiful blue eyes. I felt like I was about to faint as my knees became weak and wobbly as I was daydreaming about blue eyes until my mom interrupted me.

"Honey, we are going to be downstairs preparing breakfast if you need us. You don't want to be late for school, do you? It's your first day of high school . . . how exciting! I remember being your age . . . it was so much fun. All the learning and the extracurricular activities are what makes school . . . um . . . fun."

It was like my mom couldn't think of the best word to describe school. I don't know if high school is fun or not, but I will just have to wait and see.

Wait! Oh great, I thought my mom was teasing me about today being the first day of school. I am so not ready to go just yet. I am freaking out. "Great!" I said sarcastically out loud as my mom left and closed the door behind her. "I have to find a perfect outfit. You have to look great on your first day." Well . . . that's what I think, anyway.

Oh, and I can't wait to see Melody, Melanie, and Stanley . . . my best friends. I haven't seen them since middle school. I can't wait to tell them about my dream. Or do I tell them? I don't want to freak them out. Maybe it wouldn't scare them . . . well, I will decide on that later.

I rummaged through my closet, and I tossed jeans, shirts, jackets, and shoes all over the floor. *What a mess . . . oh well, I will clean it up later.* Just as I thought this, I looked down at the top of the pile, and I found the cutest outfit ever. I placed my outfit on the bed and tried it on in front of my mirror in the corner of my bedroom. I put on a sparkly pink top with jeans that had an embroidered butterfly on the right bottom pant leg, then I placed on my pink satin heels, and last but not least, I put on a bright pink jacket. I looked in the mirror and said, "This is perfect." I ran very fast down the stairs, with my high heels on, and rushed outside without eating breakfast. While outside, I remembered that I forgot to do something really important, and I walked back into the house.

"Thanks, Mom, for helping me feel better," I said as I gave her a hug and said goodbye. I walked down the four wide steps and walked to the side yard. I grabbed ahold of my pink bicycle and rolled it in front of our mailbox.

My mom stood at the door and said, "You're welcome, dear," as she waved her hand goodbye.

It was such a beautiful sunny day outside to ride my bike to my first day of class. I felt the orange, hot sun shining on my skin. The gentle breeze of the wind blew my hair across my face. I saw my mom's beautiful rose garden behind me as I turned around to wave goodbye to my parents.

It is not easy to ride a bike with heels, I chuckled, but I manage. I choose to wear higher shoes because I am only five-foot-two. I rode my bike two blocks down the road and turned right into the high school. "Bluesville High," the sign read; the building looked a lot bigger than the picture I saw on the internet. I soon became very nervous and anxious all at once. The school was a tall, brick building which was two stories. In front of the school, there was a tall water fountain with an angel on top. The angel was holding a pitcher, and the water was pouring out of it. There were many kids sitting near the fountain chatting with one another while waiting for school to begin. The cheerleaders were raising their pompoms in the air on the left side of the fountain, while the football players were preparing for the upcoming game on the other side.

I was worried that I would be rejected by my fellow classmates since I was kind of the new kid. My mom always told me that I was pretty, but how come none of the cute guys asked me out in middle school? I have long, straight brown hair to the middle of my back, blue eyes, and a clear complexion. Maybe one day, a cute guy will ask me out on a date.

I lifted my head up high, walked closer to the front door of the school, and locked up my bike. I went inside the school, and all of the other students were staring at me, so I just ignored them and continued walking to my first class, which was homeroom. I try not to let other students' actions bother me, but sometimes it really does hurt. Our homeroom teacher, Mrs. Anderson, passed out our class schedules. Right after that, the announcements came on, and the principal welcomed us back to another semester of learning. My entire homeroom stood up to say the Pledge of Allegiance, and after we were finished, we waited for the bell to ring.

The bell rang, and the entire class walked out of homeroom. My next class was English. My professor of English was a tall, slender man with glasses. His name was Mr. Russell, who misplaced his glasses every ten minutes, which was very funny, by the way. So, our class had a pretty good laugh every ten minutes. He handed out our textbooks, and we began working on our first assignment. The assignment was really easy, so I was done in no time. I looked up at the clock, and we had only two minutes left of class. While waiting for the bell to ring, I got my books stacked up so that I could be out the door before the wild animals, I mean, students, knocked me down in the hallway. When the bell rang, I put my English books in my locker and went to my next class. On the way to my locker, I got through the halls quite nicely, but on the way to my next class, I wasn't so lucky. In the hallway, a bunch of students kept bumping into me while rushing to get to class on time. Another two guys weren't watching where they were going, and they bumped into me, almost knocking my books right out of my arms. They almost knocked me down, too, but I caught my balance and stood back up. I had a pretty rough start so far, but the next class was where everything was going to change. My next class was math, and that is where I saw the most attractive guy that I have ever seen.

I stood for a couple of minutes by the doorway, staring at my new crush. I could not believe how incredibly handsome he was, and I bet he was very popular, too. I looked at him while he was standing there talking to another guy. He had the most beautiful blonde hair, baby blue eyes, and he was really tall. Well, taller than me, anyway. He turned his head around, facing my direction, and his smile lit up the room. He was wearing a blue shirt with a number twenty-six sports jacket and dark jeans.

I found him to be so irresistible that I began to daydream once more. I felt like I was in fantasy land or even on cloud nine. We were dressed up in old-fashioned clothing, clothes resembling what people used to wear in the Medieval era. I was dancing with him in the prettiest ball gown, but in the middle of dancing, he spun me around, and I looked down at my dress, and it was shredded. I don't know what could have caused that. I wanted to know what happened next . . . I was curious, but something happened quickly to ruin my special moment. Right in the middle of my daydream, the bell rang at the worst time ever. The shock of the loud bell popped my daydream away, and I went back to reality and started working on my algebra. As the class was coming to a close, I turned around to look at him and started to wonder if I could ever date a guy like him.

My math class was over, and I was off to lunch. I went through the line and ordered chicken nuggets, fries, and chocolate milk. I was extra thirsty, so I opened my milk and took a sip. When I got to the register, I paid for my meal. After I got out of line, I walked to the corner table where my best friends were sitting. I have not seen my friends since middle school. My friends are twins, and they do everything together. I have known them since I was six years old. The one on the right is named Melanie, and the one on the left is Melody. Melody and Melanie may look alike, but their personalities are quite different. Melanie is shy, sympathetic, and loves doing girlie things. On the other hand, her sister Melody is more of a tomboy. She likes playing sports and being outside. Melanie's long dark hair hung over her shoulders while Melody's hair was pulled back into a ponytail. Melanie was wearing a light blue jacket, a purple top, and dark jeans. Melody was wearing a red tank that read "I love sports" in black letters, and jeans that had holes in the knees, and a black cap on her head. Melanie was reading a book, and Melody was scribbling in her notebook.

As I was about to sit down, one of the most popular girls in school knocked my tray out of my hand. There went my milk, all over my nice, brand-new jeans.

"Hey! You just spilled my milk all over me," I hollered. "These are my brand-new jeans."

Melody and Melanie stopped what they were doing, and they both had their mouths wide open in shock.

This girl was dressed in a light blue cheerleader top with a dark blue skirt. Her hair was styled in a high ponytail, and her hair was curled from the hairband to the ends with tiny curls on both sides of her face. She was the most feared girl at Bluesville High. Brittany was her name, and she was the head cheerleader. She was spoiled and didn't care about anyone . . . except herself.

"Oops . . . sorry about your jeans," said Brittany. "Well, actually,

I am not really sorry. Anyway, your jeans look better this way. The chocolate gives them a nice touch," she said as she pointed down at my jeans. "What was I going to say? Oh yeah, I saw you staring at my boyfriend earlier. How dare you!"

"I wasn't staring at your boyfriend," I told her. "Today is my first day of school. I have no idea who your boyfriend is."

"Uh . . . the most attractive guy in this school. Who else?" said Brittany. "Let me refresh your memory. He's the tall guy with blonde hair that you were drooling over in math class."

How in the world did she see me looking at him? I didn't see her anywhere around, or at least, I didn't think I saw her there. I was too caught up in my romantic daydream that I didn't remember her being there. "I wasn't drooling over him," I fibbed to Brittany as I smiled at the twins.

"I want this to be really clear, and I mean it. Don't ever look at him again, or you will regret it," she said in an angry tone as she walked away.

Why would I stop looking at him just because she said I couldn't?

I grabbed the side of my jeans where the chocolate stain was and said, "Eww, this is so gross. How am I going to get this stain out? My mom is going to kill me."

"Don't worry about it," Melanie said as she handed me her napkin while I sat down next to them at the table.

"What's her problem?" I asked as I started to wipe my jeans. "I didn't do anything to her."

"Actually, I have been wondering that myself," Melody said with a slight laugh.

"She doesn't like anyone to look at her boyfriend," said Melanie.

"Just great!" I said sarcastically. "I had no idea that the guy I was looking at was dating anyone. I should have known he was taken since he was so cute."

Melody suddenly remembered something and pointed to her

sister. "Do you remember the story that was in the school's paper about Amanda?"

"Yes, I do," said Melanie.

"That poor girl had to transfer to another school, just because of Brittany."

"Oh great, that's exciting news," I said in a sarcastic way as I continued to eat the rest of my food. "By the way, what can you tell me about Brittany's boyfriend?"

I was so excited to see and talk to my friends about my crush that I forgot about my milk stain on my pants.

"Well, let me see," said Melanie. "His name is Jason Taylor. He is five-foot-eight-inches tall, as it says in last year's football booklet I found in the lost-and-found box. He has blonde hair, and he is really handsome."

"It doesn't say the last part in the booklet, does it?" Melody asked. "Don't tell me you are falling for him, too."

"I am not falling for him," said Melanie as she shook her head from side to side. "I am just describing him for Cynthia."

"Oh okay . . . sure," said Melody as if she didn't believe her sister. "Jason is on our football team. He is the quarterback for the Bluesville Angels."

"Just hearing all of this stuff about him makes him even more dreamy," I said. After that, I started to wonder how long Brittany and Jason have been dating. "How long has Jason been dating Brittany?"

Melanie and Melody both looked at each other. Both of them were unsure of who was going to answer my question.

"They have been dating for about a year now," said Melanie.

I knew Jason was dating Brittany by the scene that happened earlier, but I had no idea why he liked her so much. All I knew from looking at him was that he had blonde hair, blue eyes, and the cutest smile ever. I just wanted to find out more about him.

CHAPTER TWO

"I can't believe Brittany told me that I could not look at Jason. Who does she think she is, ordering me around like that?" I said as I sat down at our usual table at lunch with my best friend, Stanley Brown. Stanley and I have been best friends since we were in kindergarten. He is like a brother to me. I looked across the table, and Stanley was wearing a green-and-white-striped shirt with light denim jeans. His hair was brown with some strands out of place. He was picking at his fries and skimming through a sports magazine. He hasn't really been active in sports at school, but he loves watching them on television. Stanley is really smart and serious at times, but he isn't afraid to have fun or joke around. Ever since the first time I met him, I could tell him everything, even the secrets I could not tell my parents.

"Don't let Brittany's little threats bother you," said Stanley as he leaned on the table with his arms folded over his magazine. He raised his head from reading and looked directly at me. "Come on; you are so much better and nicer than her."

Melanie and Melody were also sitting at the same table with us. Melody was seated right next to Stanley. She kept tilting her head up and to the side, trying to view the parts of the magazine that Stanley wasn't covering with his arms. I could tell that Melody was a little annoyed with Stanley. I turned my head to the side to look at Melanie. Melanie was quite entertained with it all, and so was I. Melanie was trying so hard to concentrate on her horse drawing, but every time she saw her sister move, she would smile and lose focus. *I bet they laugh at each other all the time*, I thought. Melanie and I both looked at each other and smiled, trying not to burst out laughing at the situation at hand. Melanie really tried to put her focus back onto her drawing of a horse, but every couple of minutes, she would lose focus and glance right back at her sister.

"I think Brittany is just jealous of you," said Melody as she looked up from the magazine.

"Yeah," said Melanie. "She probably thinks Jason is going to fall desperately in love with you."

"Hey guys, you are so funny," I said. "How could Brittany be jealous of a little girl like me? I mean . . . she is a popular cheerleader, has a cute boyfriend, and rules the school." I kept thinking over and over again. Could my friends be right about Brittany? Does she really think I am going to steal her boyfriend away? "I am not sure if your comments are true about Brittany, but it doesn't hurt to guess, right?" As I was saying this, I couldn't help but think, *are my friends right, or is Brittany going to make my life miserable?*

As the bell rang, Stanley asked silently, "Have you looked at Jason since the incident with Brittany?"

"Yes, it's kind of hard not to . . . considering we are in the same math class," I whispered. "I wonder what she is going to do to me when she catches me looking at my crush."

"I don't know," said Stanley in a worried tone. "Just be careful; try not to look at him. I don't want to see my best friend get hurt."

I was standing by the doorway of my algebra class, waiting for the teacher to arrive. In the corner of my eye, I saw my crush and Brittany walking toward me. They were holding hands and smiling. To me, they were dressed so perfectly, like a couple of models walking down a long runway. Brittany's hair was flat-ironed straight, which draped right over her shoulders. She was wearing a white dress with a cherry in the bottom left corner of her skirt. Jason was wearing a blue plaid shirt and white pants. Neither of them had a hair out of place. As soon as Brittany saw me, her face went from a smile to a mean grin.

"Oh no," I said silently as she caught me looking at Jason. *What am I going to do now?* I thought. Jason and Brittany stopped right in front of me and knocked my books right out of my hands.

"Oops, I am so sorry," Brittany said as she left Jason standing alone as she walked away with a smirk-like grin on her face.

Jason kneeled down and started helping me pick up my books. "I am so sorry that Brittany did this to you," said Jason. "She gets jealous when other girls look at me. I will have a talk with her later and try to get her to stop picking on you."

"Thanks, Jason," I replied. "I hope we can all get along and be friends instead of being enemies."

"Yes," said Jason. "I would like that very much."

However, that was not even the case. Things got even worse after Jason had a talk with Brittany. One day at lunch, she placed a tray of food on my seat. I did not even know it was there until I sat down. I felt so gross afterward; it was like having a pie slammed in your face, but worse, being that the food was on my bottom. I was wearing a skirt that day too, and the food was dripping down my leg. I was so embarrassed; the school principal had to call my mom to bring me fresh clothes. Another time, she placed a banana peel by my locker. Guess what embarrassing thing happened next? You're right. I slipped on it while wearing high heels and fell flat on my face. My eyes, arms, and legs were bruised for weeks. The next day, somehow, Brittany got my locker combination number. While I was in class, she snuck into my locker and placed a fake spider in it. When I finally got to my locker, I screamed so loud that the whole school probably heard me. After all of these incidents that occurred, the counselor found me in the hall and asked me if I wanted to talk to him about it.

"Not really," I told him, but I went anyway.

"How long has Brittany been bothering you?" he asked as he sat on the stool behind his desk while I sat on the couch in his small office.

"She has been bothering me nonstop for a couple of weeks now," I told him.

"That's not good," said the counselor. "Please continue. Talking about it is always the first step. You will definitely feel better afterward."

I told him about her knocking my books out of my hands, the lunch-tray incident, and the fake spider in my locker. It seemed like I was in there forever. After I told him everything, the counseling session was over, and I still didn't feel any better.

I was on my way to gym class, and I had no idea what was in store for me. It was our day to play basketball. As usual, I was picked last. The team captains were Brittany and another cheerleader named Jennifer. I was so glad that I was not on Brittany's team, but that didn't matter.

As Brittany and her team huddled, the team captain spoke of something that made all of the other cheerleaders laugh . . . I sure hoped it is not about me. Or could it be about someone else? Yes, that could be it. I saw Brittany break out of the huddle as she walked to a ball on the gym floor. What are these girls up to? I was not sure if I wanted to find out . . . I was scared out of my mind.

Brittany was first, of course, and then the rest of them followed. They all started throwing basketballs at me. A couple of the basketballs hit my arms; others hit my legs. The last one hit my eyebrow, and I fell backward onto the floor. My gym teacher had to call the ambulance because I was hurt so bad, in a lot of pain, and couldn't move a muscle. The principal called both of my parents while they were still at work. My mom called my brother and sister to come to the hospital. My mom, dad, and siblings were on their way, as I was told by my gym teacher. I could not believe how each torture from Brittany got worse and worse as each day went by. *At least*, I thought to myself, *I am finally safe.*

CHAPTER THREE

There was a loud siren coming to the front of my school. They were coming for me. I wasn't unconscious or anything, but I was just afraid to move. I was not going to move until the paramedics and firefighters checked me out first. I heard many loud sounds of clopping footsteps from the firefighters as they were running down the hall. Their footsteps became softer as they entered, and one of the guys placed an oxygen mask on me, another checked my pulse, and the third guy checked to see if I had any broken bones. I felt like I was in heaven. They were the three most cutest guys I have ever seen—well, except for my crush.

"Does this girl have any broken bones?" my gym teacher asked.

"Ma'am, I felt her bones in her legs and arms, and her right leg and left arm appear to be broken," said one of the paramedics.

"Oh no," said my gym teacher. "I hope her injuries are not serious."

The second cutest paramedic said, "We will x-ray her at the hospital just to be sure."

The three men lifted me up gently and placed me on a stretcher. They strapped me down, which made me feel like a mouse trapped in a mousetrap. They raised the stretcher up and rolled me across the gym. As I got farther away from the basketball court, I heard the teacher fussing at Brittany for what she had done. If it weren't for her, I would not be going to the hospital right now. I had no idea what punishment was in store for Brittany, and I know this is bad to say, but I could not wait to find out. I mean, she deserves everything she gets for what happened to me.

I did start to enjoy the ride on the stretcher, but I was tired of being strapped in. We traveled down the long hallway, passing alumni photos, student artwork, trophies, and student event papers. As we got closer to the main entrance of Bluesville High, one of the paramedics let go of my stretcher and ran to open the door. The other two paramedics pulled me through the door, and we were outside. The cool, gentle breeze felt so good on my face. They carefully took me down the twelve steps slowly, one step at a time, until we reached the last one.

"Boy," I said, "I sure felt like a human basketball today." I started to giggle. The three men were glad to see that I was happy, and at that moment, a smile appeared on each of their faces.

We walked by the beautiful fountain with the angel pouring a pitcher of water into the pond below. Every time I walked by the angel, it gave me a calm and relaxing feeling. I just felt like I was going to be all right. I just knew it, somehow.

The paramedics stopped, and one of them opened the back door of the ambulance. The three guys lifted me in and checked me over again. One of the paramedics was waiting in the ambulance when we arrived. Two of the paramedics stayed in the back with me while the other two jumped out of the back of the truck and walked to the front of the ambulance. The driver opened the door, sat in the car, and started the ignition. He turned on his siren, and off we went.

Our little neighborhood is one of the prettiest I have ever seen. I looked out the small window on the ambulance door and saw many large trees that looked like they reached and touched the sky. Then I noticed that the trees appeared to be a little wet. It must have been raining while I was in the gym because a rainbow just suddenly appeared in the sky. It was such a beautiful picture.

After I saw the rainbow, I started to cry because I was in so much pain. The paramedics told me that we were almost there. We finally arrived near the hospital. It was a short drive, but it seemed like it took much longer. The hospital building was on the right side of the road. The paramedic that was driving turned on his right blinker and entered onto a small path that led to the back way of the hospital, which was where the emergency room was located. The paramedic stopped and parked the ambulance in front of the emergency room. He opened the front door, then walked to the back door of the ambulance to help lift me out. The four men worked together and got my stretcher placed on the ground.

The men rolled me into the emergency room while passing two bright red rose bushes. The rose bushes were bordering a small pathway leading to the entrance. As we approached the door, I saw my mom pacing back and forth, waiting for me to arrive.

"I am so glad my baby girl is finally here so she can start to recover and feel better," said my mom.

I could not believe how many people were in this room. I saw young children, teenagers like me, adults, and seniors. By looking at all of these people who were ahead of me, I thought I would never be seen. I felt like I was in the emergency room for ten hours, but it was only two hours. After about two hours and thirty minutes of long waiting, they finally called my name. All I was thinking about at that very moment was that I wanted to get better as soon as possible so that I could get to see my crush again.

The nurses rolled my stretcher down the hallway, and I saw many people who were hurt and sick like me. The first elderly lady we passed was sitting in her chair, looking down at the floor. I was wondering why no one was keeping her company. I almost cried when she looked up at me with a sad look in her eye. I gave her the biggest smile I could, and she smiled back. It feels great to see a cheerful expression from someone even if I don't know them. A smile is simple and contagious, and it can make someone who is depressed go from sad to happy in an instant. I was so glad that I could make someone smile today.

In the next room, we passed was a young man watching soccer on television. He appeared to be very healthy in the short second that I saw him, but he was very loud. The nurses that were roaming the halls were covering their ears when they walked past his door. He must be a big fan of soccer since he was yelling at his team for missing their goal.

While being pulled down the hall, I saw many photos of the doctors and staff that work in the building.

Farther down the hall, I saw a young blond-haired girl who looked like she was in her late twenties, talking to her mom. Her mom was sitting in a chair beside her daughter. I could not hear much of their conversation, but it sounded like they were discussing baby names.

The nurse turned my stretcher to the left, and we waited for the elevator door to open. Another nurse carrying a needle tray stepped out of the elevator. This nurse was dressed in an aqua green shirt and pants and had a mouth mask hanging around her neck like a necklace. She wasn't really friendly, but I guess she had to get to the lab very quickly. My nurse pushed my stretcher into the elevator and pressed number three. All I could hear was the light sound of pop music coming from the top front corner of the elevator. The light buttons lit up as we reached each floor. We finally reached level three, and the elevator stopped.

The elevator doors opened, and two other nurses came to help pull my stretcher out. They turned right, and I arrived at room 310. When you first walk in, there is a nice sized bathroom close to the door. The tub was on one side, and the toilet and sink were on the other. The room has a little hallway that goes to the bedroom. This room had a bed on the back wall and a television set hanging on the front wall. In the right back corner of the room, there were two brown wooden chairs and a small table. This room appeared to be nicer than I thought it would be.

The nurses picked me up and placed me gently on the bed. They showed me all of the different gadgets and explained to me how each of them worked.

"If you need anything, please let us know," said one of the nurses. "We are here to help make you as comfortable as possible."

While they exited the door, I turned on the television to see what was on that was interesting enough to watch.

The same nurse from before came in and said, "The doctor is going to come in to x-ray your whole body to see if your bones are broken."

"Okay, that's fine," I said as she went back into the hallway to start scheduling for my x-ray.

I started to flip through the channels. Nothing was on except the news, sports, and a shopping channel. I wasn't interested in watching the news or sports, so I put it on the shopping channel. The lady on the screen was trying to convince the viewers to buy a ring, then earrings, and even a bracelet. Each of these items was shown about ten minutes apart. I wanted to buy all of them, but they were way too expensive for me to purchase. But the show was really entertaining to watch, anyway.

About thirty minutes later, the doctor came in with the x-ray machine. It was an x-ray machine on wheels.

"I have never seen an x-ray machine like this one before," I told the doctor.

I looked up at the doctor and noticed his features. He had short brown hair, green eyes, a round face, with a mustache above his lips. He grabbed a pen from out of his shirt pocket and picked up his clipboard from the tray that was on top of the x-ray machine. The doctor looked down at his clipboard and started writing. I wasn't sure what he was writing, but I hoped it wasn't anything bad. The doctor placed his clipboard on my bed and walked back to the x-ray machine that was in front of my bed. As he started unraveling and untangling the cords, he started to speak.

"The doctors and I all worked together to devise a machine that would take x-rays of patients in their own rooms, so we would not have to move a patient into another room. So, we bring the x-ray machine to them, which helps make it easier on the patient, and plus, we get the results quickly. I am sorry, where are my manners," said the doctor. He wiped his hand on his shirt and held out his hand. "I did not introduce myself to you. I am Dr. Barnes. But you can call me Michael."

"Nice to meet you, Dr. Barnes," I replied as I shook his hand with the arm that wasn't sore. With all of the pain that I am in, I forgot that the doctor told me that he wanted me to call him by his first name. I have never been on a first-name base with a doctor, dentist, or anyone. It just felt weird, so I just nervously swallowed my saliva and coughed. "I mean, Michael."

The same young, red-headed nurse appeared at the doorway of my room. "Do you need any assistance to take Ms. Adams' x-rays?"

"Yes! I would love some help," said Dr. Barnes. "I was just about to call a nurse. Thanks for arriving in the nick of time."

The red-headed nurse walked from the door to my bed with a big smile on her face. "Hi, Ms. Cynthia Adams. I would like to introduce myself. My name is Amy."

"Nice to meet you, Amy. You can just call me Cynthia."

Amy and Doctor Barnes lifted the x-ray machine over me. He took about two of my whole body, three of my arms, and three of my legs. He attached the x-rays onto the board in front of me to study them. The doctor stood there and looked at them for at least ten minutes.

"Cynthia, I am going to take these to the x-ray room down the hall and study them a bit further," said Dr. Barnes.

As he left, I continued watching television. Amy and another nurse came in, and moved the x-ray device, and cleaned up a bit. It was Thursday, six o'clock in the evening, and an older lady came in to give me my dinner. I opened the tan pot, and inside was meatloaf and green beans. They also gave me a side of peaches and a cup of lime gelatin for dessert.

At seven thirty-five, the doctor came in to report his findings. "Sorry dear, I have some bad news to tell you. It appears that your right leg and left arm are broken. I am going to place a cast on your arm and leg so that they can heal faster." He gave me a pink cast for my arm and a blue one for my leg.

"When did they start this?" I asked curiously. "I never knew that casts came in different colors."

"Well, many of our patients got tired of the plain tan and white casts, so our hospital supplies company started dying them a couple of years ago. Since they have started dying them, our patients have been a lot happier," said Dr. Barnes. My doctor raised my right leg in the air and placed on my cast. He tightened the cast around my arm, and then he picked up a shot dispenser and a vial that was on the counter in front of the room. "I am going to give you medicine that will make you sleepy to relieve the pain."

Not too long after he gave me the medicine, I fell asleep and started to dream. My dream felt so real, like I was doing it in real life, if only it were real. My mom and I were at the bridal shop called Rose's Bridal.

My mom said to me, "This bridal shop has been here for nearly twenty years, and it's still in business. I even bought my first wedding dress here when I married your father."

"Really, Mom?" My eyes perked up. "I am so excited that I am going to buy a dress from the same bridal shop that you did."

"Yes, I am really excited, too," said my mom as a tear slid down her cheek. "My little girl is all grown up."

We both turned around and started searching for dresses. Oh, the dresses were so beautiful. They were all so different, and the material and design were so exquisite. Some had ruffles, others had lace and flowers, while other ones had so much color and glitter that they looked like they were made directly from a rainbow.

I tried on a dress that was sparkly pink on top that had flower designs throughout the dress with ruffles near the bottom. As soon as I put on the dress, I knew it was the right one for me.

"Mom, this is the dress that I want to be married in next month."

"Okay, honey," said my mom. "Are you sure that you don't want to look at more dresses?"

"No, I like this one," I replied. "It is just perfect."

I looked in the long mirror in front of me and twirled around three times. "I can't wait to see what I look like in this dress with my hair and makeup done."

I think my mom knew exactly how special this dress was to me. I could tell by the happy tear that ran down her face as she watched me spin around. "I am sure you will look exquisite. You always do. Jason is going to love this dress."

I woke up, and my pain medication wore off, and it was already ten o'clock the next morning. I felt refreshed and tired but still in pain. I hope Dr. Barnes or one of the nurses comes in so that they can give me my pain medicine.

I wonder if my dream was true or not? Am I really going to marry him? Or is it another guy named Jason? This dream is probably too good to be true, but a girl can dream, can't she? Too bad I could not see what he looked like, but I am in too much pain to go back to sleep.

At eleven o'clock, Amy came in with my lunch.

"Good morning, dear. How are you feeling today?"

I am not sure why nurses ask this question all the time. If I was feeling good, I wouldn't be in here right now. But I didn't want to appear crabby or rude, so I tried to sit up in bed. But when I tried to straighten up, the pain in my bones made it impossible to move. I felt as stiff as a tree that was chopped to the ground. When I gave up trying to straighten up, I spoke to the nurse. "I am okay, but my medicine wore off. I am still in a lot of pain."

"Okay, sweetie," said Amy. "I will have the doctor come in to check on you." She pulled up the bendable table that was attached to the bed and placed it in front of me. She placed the tray on my little table. "Enjoy your lunch," she said as she smiled and walked out of the room.

I lifted the lid of my food container. Inside was a turkey sandwich with potato chips, salad, and grape juice. *Boy, did they give me a lot of food*, I thought. My sandwich looked really delicious. I looked over at my salad with the leafy green lettuce, tomatoes, cheese, and cucumbers. I haven't eaten a salad in a few weeks. I was so hungry. Just looking at my meal made my mouth water, so I started to eat.

Later, back at the high school, right as the last bell of the day rang, Jason ran out of his construction class door and went straight to his locker. His locker was number 217 on J hall, which was nine lockers in front of Cynthia's. Cynthia's locker is number 226, and it is in the best hall of the school. Jason opened his locker and picked up his English, math, and history books to take home with him. He walked down J hall, passing many lockers and classrooms.

In one of the rooms farther down the hall, a guy in a red shirt wearing a cap shouted, "Good luck, man, with the football game next Friday!"

"Thanks, man!" said Jason. "I really appreciate it."

Jason wasn't worried about the game. He knew he would do well, but he wanted to leave for his destination right away before he ran into Brittany.

Jason walked by a couple more classrooms and turned into a small hallway that led to the student parking lot. He opened the door, stepped outside, and continued walking down a small pathway that had two neatly trimmed evergreen bushes on both edges of the sidewalk.

Jason couldn't believe how hot it was outside. He could feel the heat of the sun touching the skin on his face. He stopped to look up at the sun while wondering why the weather was so excruciating. With his hand slanted downward over his forehead, he tried to cover his eyes from the beaming rays.

The temperature must have been in the nineties.

Jason wiped his face with his hand, but that didn't help much. He was outside only for a few minutes, but he was already burning up. The sweat just rolled down his arms as a cloud pours rain onto the earth.

Jason finally reached his blue Mustang GT. He opened the door, sat down, and put the key into the ignition to turn on the air conditioner. While still holding his books in his left hand, he gently placed them on the seat next to his. Jason's car was very tidy, with his school books in the front seat, a coffee mug in the drink holder, and a sports cap in the back. His jacket was still wrapped over his right arm. He tossed his twenty-six football jacket in the back seat, and it landed roughly over his cap.

He placed his gear in reverse and looked both ways behind him. While also looking in the rearview mirrors, he slowly started to back out. There was another car coming behind him, and he stopped. He waited until the car passed and backed up again, just when the buses started to leave.

The buses started to drive past him, and Jason shouted, "Come on you silly buses. I was just about to pull out. I have an important place to be before it closes." Then he started to laugh and said, "This is going to take forever. I am never going to get out of here."

One by one, the eight buses pulled out in front of him. After all of the eight buses left, Jason was free to go. Jason drove straight ahead, passing a large oak tree and that beautiful angel situated above the fountain. He looked at the water and noticed that someone put soap in the fountain. He smiled while wondering who pulled the prank. But even with the soap in the fountain, the water glistened so beautifully when the sun touched it.

"One day, I am going to propose to my girlfriend at that spot. That day will be the most romantic night of my life."

Jason drove down the street toward the hospital, driving past people walking on the sidewalk, riding bikes, and kids playing in the playground. Jason came upon a red light and stopped his car. Jason turned the music up and started patting on the steering wheel.

"Oh great, this light is taking forever to change," said Jason as he looked at his watch. "I guess I am not supposed to see Cynthia today." *Why do these things always happen to me?* he pondered. *If Brittany found out that I was going to see Cynthia, she would go berserk. Actually, it would be funny to see Brittany go berserk,* Jason thought as he started to chuckle. "Ugh, this annoying stoplight. I am never going to get there in time."

He glanced over and saw a young couple, who were in their thirties, feeding the fish in a nearby pond. The man placed his knees on the ground while his wife gave him the fish food. The man threw the food into the pond, and a medium-sized fish appeared out of the water and looked straight up at the man. What a surprise that man saw. The fish's appearance from out of nowhere was unexpected, and it scared the man, causing him to jump. Jason saw the whole thing, and he laughed so hard when he saw that man's facial expression.

The light finally turned green, and Jason drove forward.

The hospital was near, on the right side of the street. He switched on his right blinker, looked both ways, and merged into the right lane. Jason turned off his blinker and drove until he reached the entrance of the hospital. He arrived at the entrance, turned right, and drove down a small, dark shady road that was enclosed by many large Evergreen trees. The road became narrow, the trees were slowly fading behind him, and a large parking lot appeared. The parking lot was full, so he drove around until he noticed a couple leaving. Jason waited until the couple got into their car and drove off. He parked in that parking space in the middle row, and he rushed out of his car.

Jason walked up to the main entrance. The sliding doors blew wide open, and a calming breeze of cool air from the air conditioner blew on his face. The breeze felt so good to him since it was ninety degrees outside. He walked through the sliding doors, and he took a look around the room. He smelled the hot, fresh caramel coffee in the corner of the waiting room. The smell of the fresh caramel coffee tempted Jason to buy a cup.

He walked up to the stand and asked, "How much for one of your caramel coffees? It smells delicious."

The guy behind the kiosk said, "For one cup of caramel coffee, the price is three dollars and fifty cents."

Jason reached into his pocket and placed four dollars on the counter.

"That will be fifty cents cash back," said the coffee owner.

"You can keep the change," said Jason.

He turned around while holding his coffee and noticed all of the people waiting to be seen by a doctor. He couldn't believe the number of people in the waiting room. Jason took a sip of his coffee and continued to look around the hospital.

Near the entrance door on the right was a small gift shop. It didn't look like an ordinary gift shop you would find in the mall, but Jason decided to take a look around. Hanging from the ceiling were get-well balloons, cards placed neatly in racks, magazines on shelves, stuffed animals, and jewelry by the counter. The jewelry tray that caught Jason's eye was the one on the counter next to the register. He stared at the bracelets until he found the perfect one.

The bracelet that caught Jason's eye had shiny pink beads with a butterfly charm attached to it. This one was extra special; it was the only one that glistened in the case..

"Oh, she would love this one," Jason said while pointing at the bracelet. "It is just perfect. How much does this one cost?"

The lady behind the counter said, "The total of this bracelet would be ten dollars."

"Okay," said Jason. "I will take it."

The sales clerk wrapped it and placed the bracelet into a small box. She cut a piece of ribbon, and wrapped it around the box, and said, "Is this gift for your girlfriend?"

Jason thought the sales clerk was being a little nosy. It was really none of her business who was receiving the gift. But, he didn't want to appear impolite, so he answered her anyway. "No. I am giving this gift to a friend who goes to my school. I kind of owe her this present since my girlfriend is responsible for her coming into this hospital in the first place. I feel sort of responsible and guilty at the same time. I did not know my girlfriend was going to treat her so unkindly."

"You know," said the sales clerk, "it's not really your fault. Your girlfriend is the one to blame, not you."

Jason looked at the white name tag on the sales clerk's shirt, which read, "Michelle."

"Thank you, Michelle," said Jason. "It was really nice talking to you. I feel a lot better now than I did before I came into this hospital."

"You're welcome," said Michelle. "I am so glad I could help."

Jason picked up the present and left the gift shop.

Jason walked up to the front desk and asked, "What is Cynthia Adams' room number?"

The front desk lady was not friendly like the lady in the gift shop. She was an average-sized woman with gray hair and glasses. Her glasses kept sliding down her nose, so every few seconds, she would push them back up. The whole time she was searching on her computer, a smile didn't appear on her face. Jason was wondering why this lady was so serious. A thought occurred to him; maybe she was a sad and lonely woman. After about five minutes had passed, the lady finally found Cynthia's room number on her computer.

"Young man, Cynthia Adams is in room 310, on the third floor."

"Thank you," said Jason.

Jason walked to the right and passed the lady that Cynthia smiled at when she first arrived at the hospital. Jason backed up and smiled at the elderly lady. She looked really lonely sitting in a chair by the front wall with her face gazing at the floor. She could sense someone by the doorway, and she lifted her head up to look at Jason. Her shiny gray strands fell back in place, and a big smile appeared on her face. Jason felt sorry for her, so he just decided to walk into her room to give her a hug.

"I am glad someone came to visit me today," said the elderly lady. "I get so lonely every day; no one here I can really talk to. My family is so busy with their lives; they forget to come and visit me."

"May I ask you your name?" said Jason.

"My name is Meredith Baker."

"Such a nice name," said Jason. "May I ask how old you are?"

"Why son, you don't ask a lady her age," said Meredith with a slight laugh. "But since you were so polite in asking. I will tell you. I am seventy-two years old."

Jason was really fascinated by how old fashioned this lady was. She kind of reminded him of his grandma; she is a good, old-fashioned woman herself.

"You really look good for your age," said Jason.

"Well, thank you, young man," said Meredith. "May I ask what your name is, son?"

"My name is Jason Taylor, and I am in tenth grade."

"Nice to meet you," said Meredith. "I hope I can see you again."

"It was nice to meet you, ma'am," said Jason as he got up from his chair and walked to the door. Subsequently, a thought entered his mind as he lifted his hand up in the air and turned around. "Have you seen a young girl on a stretcher come by here recently?"

"Yes, I did see her," said Meredith. "I saw her come by here earlier today. She smiled at me as you did."

"That's the girl I am going to visit after I visit you," said Jason. "Her name is Cynthia Adams. My girlfriend is the reason why she is in the hospital."

"Oh my," said Meredith. "What happened to her, Jason?"

"Oh . . . a bunch of girls and my girlfriend threw basketballs at her, just because she was looking at me," said Jason. "I know that sounds ridiculous, but my girlfriend gets really jealous of things like that."

"That's terrible, Jason," said Meredith.

"I know, but that's the way my girlfriend is," said Jason. "I try reasoning with her to get her to stop picking on other girls, but she just doesn't listen to me. She'd rather make decisions on her own than take someone else's advice."

"Well . . . she doesn't sound like a very nice girl, Jason," said Meredith. "I wish you could meet my granddaughter. She is about your age. She is such a sweet and beautiful girl."

"Yeah, I would like to meet your granddaughter one day," said Jason. Even though Jason didn't want another girl to have a crush on him since all of the other girls at school are crazy for him. But, he still wanted to meet the girl. She sounded really nice by the way Meredith was describing her. Then, he thought, maybe he could just be friends with the girl even though he was still with Brittany. Maybe Brittany wouldn't mind, but in his heart, he knew she would.

"Yes, that would be great," said Meredith. "I don't want to keep you from seeing your friend. Well, you go up and see her."

"I really enjoyed talking to you," said Jason.

"Me too, sweetheart," said Meredith. "Thanks for giving an old lady some company."

Jason walked out of Meredith's room and turned to the right. The young girl that was pregnant was not there anymore. That room was now being occupied by a young boy laying on his bed with his leg high in the air. The little boy looked about seven, maybe eight, with short red hair, freckles, and a green cast on his left leg. The little boy looked up from playing his video game and waved at Jason, and Jason waved back. Suddenly, Jason heard the clomping footsteps of a woman wearing high heels coming near him. He backed up, not knowing which way she was going to turn. Quickly, she walked right in front of Jason while almost stepping on his foot. She was holding a drink and a sandwich and walked right into the room of the little boy.

"Here you go, sweetie. I have something for you to eat." She placed the tray in front of the little boy.

"Thank you, Mommy. I am so hungry," cried the little boy. The little boy picked up his cheese sandwich and started to eat.

"You're welcome, sweetheart," said the boy's mom.

The boy's mom looked at Jason. "I am sorry, young man. I didn't see you there. I hope I didn't knock you down. I was in a rush trying to get my child something to eat."

"It's okay, ma'am," said Jason. "Don't worry about it."

Jason continued on, walking straight until he approached the elevator and turned left. One of the elevators was open already, so he ran as fast as he could before it closed. He got in just in time. Jason pressed number three, and it took him to the third floor. The elevator stopped, and Jason stepped out. He saw a lady standing behind a counter filing documents while talking to a nurse with red hair. Both of the nurses were giggling. Jason stood there for a moment, trying to figure out if he was supposed to sign in to see Cynthia.

"Do you want to hear something funny that happened to me?" said the nurse with red hair.

"Yes, I do," said the other nurse. "I bet it isn't as funny as my story."

"Oh, but it is," said the nurse with red hair. "I can't believe I am actually going to tell you this. The other day I went to lunch with my friends. We were all having a good time, and some weird dude came up to me and started flirting with me. I had no idea who he was. I was so nervous that I spilled my drink all over my lap. I looked at my friends and they were laughing at me. I was so embarrassed; it was like, I don't want to mention it. Okay, it was like I peed my pants. I just laughed it off with the girls even though I wanted to hide under the table."

"Boy, that's even more hilarious than my story," said the other nurse. "Did you ever find out who this guy was?"

"Yes, I did. This guy that was apparently trying to flirt with me was a guy that I used to hang out with."

"Oh my gosh!" said the other nurse as she placed her hand over her mouth. "Really? You didn't recognize him?"

Meanwhile, Jason paced to his right and to his left as the conversation was continuing. He had too much on his mind to listen. He wasn't sure if he was supposed to check in with the nurses, but he didn't really want to bother them since they were laughing and having such a good time.

He stopped pacing and noticed that room 310 was on the right side of the hall, so he continued in that direction. Jason walked down to room 310 and knocked on the door.

I heard a knock at the door of my room.

"Who is it?"

"It's Jason. Can I come in and visit you for a while?"

Oh my goodness, I could not believe that Jason is behind my door and wants to hang out with me. I was really excited and shocked at the same time. What is he doing here? I never thought he would be the one visiting me. Maybe Melody, Melanie, or Stanley, but definitely not Jason.

"Hold on, one moment, Jason," I hollered. I reached across to the little table next to me and grabbed my brush. I brushed my hair to make it look pretty for Jason. I tucked my hair around my ears and said, "Okay, Jason. You may come in now. Please excuse the way I look. I haven't felt good."

Jason turned the knob on the door and walked in, saying, "You look pretty; don't worry about it. How are you feeling today?"

I can't believe he said that I looked pretty. I didn't feel pretty at all, but it was nice that he said it. I had a little trouble letting my eyes get in contact with his. I just couldn't bear the thought of him seeing me like this. In the corner of my eye, I got a glimpse of him standing by the doorway, and he looked so handsome in his blue shirt and dark jeans. His blue shirt made his eyes pop, which made him look even more dreamy. After I saw him, I finally got the courage to talk to him.

"I am still in pain, but I will be okay," I told him with a smile. Suddenly, my worries about my appearance just somehow vanished. I think just having the opportunity to see him made me happy and able to forget about the way I looked.

"I want to ask you something," said Jason.

"You can ask me anything you want," I replied. In my head, I was thinking, *is he going to ask me out?* This is the moment I have been waiting for all my life, but I look just plain awful. Ugh . . . my worries have come back.

"Do you know Meredith?" asked Jason. "She is such a sweet lady."

Well, it wasn't the question I was hoping for, but I said, "I have not had the pleasure to meet her yet. Who is Meredith, by the way?"

"Oh," said Jason. "I think you saw her on the way to your room when you first came here. She is the one that looks so lonely. I went in and talked to her for a few minutes."

"Yes, I did see her," I said. "I felt so bad for her. I wanted to give her a hug, but I was strapped to my stretcher."

The visualization that Jason and I had of me being strapped to a stretcher made us burst out laughing.

"Oh, I almost forgot," said Jason. "I have a little present for you."

"Aw, that was really . . . sweet of you," I said. "You did not have to get me anything."

Jason was about to reach into his pocket, and at that same moment, my mom walked in on us. I could tell right then and there that my mom was going to embarrass me.

"Oh! Hi, baby girl," said my mom, in shock. "I didn't know you had company."

Jason stood up to introduce himself. "Hi, Mrs. Adams. My name is Jason Taylor."

After he introduced himself to my mom, he awkwardly sat back down in the chair beside me.

"Oh, so this is the guy I have heard so much about," said my mom. "I didn't know your crush was visiting you today. It is so nice to meet you, Jason."

I was so embarrassed. I thought I was going to die. I looked at Jason, and his face was red, too. I began to daydream, and I started to think about how cute Jason looked sitting there listening to my mom. I snapped out of my little daydream and started to focus. Something felt weird, but I kept trying to figure it out. Then, it just hit me. How did my mom know that I had a crush on Jason? I haven't had the chance to tell her about him. The only people I have told were Melanie and Melody. My friends wouldn't have told a secret as big as that to my mom. I was thinking about asking her about it right then and there, but I decided not to. I didn't want to make the situation more embarrassing than it already was.

"Well, I guess I will leave you two alone," my mom said as she smiled at me. "I will come back to visit you a little later."

"Okay, I will see you later," I told her.

My mom walked out the door.

"Jason, I am so sorry about that. My mom kind of says whatever is on her mind. That was so embarrassing."

"Yeah . . . that was a little embarrassing, but I am over it now."

I could not believe how cool he was. I thought he would freak out about what just happened.

"What were we doing before we got interrupted?" Jason asked as he was about to reach for my hand. He raised his index finger up. "Oh, I remember. I was about to give you the present that I bought for you."

Now it was coming to that perfect moment with Jason and me. Jason put his right hand into his pocket and brought out a small package wrapped with a bow. It was the prettiest gift box ever. The box was bright pink, and the ribbon was light pink with sparkles.

"Oh, Jason, the box is so pretty," I said with a giggle. "How did you know pink was my favorite color?"

Jason's eyes began to brighten as he thought about what he was going to say. "On the first day of school, you wore a sparkly pink top with butterfly jeans and pink satin heels. I have never seen a girl wear so much pink. The bright pink of your clothes made you stand out from the rest of the girls. So that is how I remembered your favorite color was pink."

Wow! I felt like I was in heaven. He made that sound so romantic. What? Wait a minute! Did he just say I stood out from the other girls? I started to get really nervous that I couldn't quit smiling.

"Open the present," Jason said with excitement. "I want to see if you like what's inside."

I started to untie the ribbon very carefully and placed it on the side of my bed.

Jason picked up my brush and started to brush my hair. He wrapped my hair into a ponytail as I opened the box. I took off the lid, and inside was the most beautiful pink and opal bracelet with a dangling butterfly charm. The little bit of sunlight coming through the window made my bracelet sparkle. I wrapped it around my wrist, and it looked so beautiful.

"Thank you so much, Jason. I really love this bracelet. This is one of the best presents that anyone has ever given me."

"You're welcome," said Jason. "I have to go practice for our football game next Friday. I don't want the coach to fuss at me. See you later, darling."

"Ah, I can't believe I am going to miss the biggest game of the year. Can you please record it for me?"

"Okay, I will see what I can do," said Jason. "The next time I visit, we can watch it together."

"So . . . it is a date, then?" I asked.

"No, it's just two friends watching a game together," said Jason. Jason left and closed the door behind him.

"Jason is never going to ask me out or admit that he has a crush on me," I sighed. I quickly took off my bracelet and placed it back into the box.

My mom came back into my room and asked, "Did Jason leave already? What happened?"

I didn't know how to answer her second question. The only answer I could think of was that Jason didn't like me as much as I liked him. I am so thrilled that I got to see him and receive this beautiful bracelet from him. I was just hoping he would ask me out, too. I knew he was still dating Brittany, so in my heart, I knew he wouldn't ask me out, but a girl can dream, right? Just the thought of saying this out loud made me too nervous, so I just said, "Mom, he left early because he had football practice today."

"Oh, okay," said my mom as she walked to the chair that was closest to my bed. My mom's eyes came across the package. "Who gave you this cute little present?" She picked up the box and took off the lid. "This packaging is just so pretty and so perfect for you. Whoever gave you this must know you quite well." She looked inside the box. "This bracelet is quite lovely."

"It's the most wonderful gift that I have ever received," I said. "It's from Jason."

"That was so sweet and nice of him to give you a gift," said my mom.

"Mom, I have a question for you," I said.

"Sure, honey," said my mom. "You can ask me anything. What's on your mind?"

"I am kind of embarrassed to ask you this," I said. "But, how did you find out that I had a crush on Jason? I don't remember telling you anything about him."

"Oh, that," said my mom as she leaned back in her chair. "It all started when I came to check on you while you were sleeping. I know, I should have told you I was here, but you looked so peaceful lying there, so I let you sleep. Then as I was reading a magazine with a flashlight in the dark, I heard you mumbling. I thought you were having a nightmare. So, I got up to feel your head to see if you had a temperature, which you didn't, then I started to hear your words clearer."

"What was I saying, Mom?" I asked.

"You said that Jason was so cute, and he had the most beautiful eyes you have ever seen," said my mom.

"I really said that? Oh, how embarrassing. I am glad that no one else heard me. Did I say anything else?"

"Yes, actually you did," said my mom. "I don't remember all of it, but you said something about a dress and getting your makeup done. I am not sure what you mean by that, but maybe you do."

I certainly knew what she was talking about. My mom heard parts of my dream that I had last night. I was just hoping she didn't hear anything more.

"So, that's how I knew about Jason," said my mom. "I just saw a cute guy that had beautiful eyes in your room, and I automatically thought it was Jason. I guess I shouldn't have said that in front of him. I am so sorry. I didn't mean to embarrass you."

"It's okay, Mom," I told her. "Don't worry about it."

Amy came in to give me my six o'clock dinner. She had the brightest smile on her face. "I saw a cute boy come in here earlier today. Is he your boyfriend?"

"Oh . . . I wish he was . . . we would make a very cute couple," I said without thinking. I can't believe I actually said that out loud. My cheeks started to get red as a rose blooming in a garden.

"Enjoy your meal," said Amy as she placed the tray in front of me. "It's pasta night at the hospital."

"Yum, my favorite," I said. I opened the lid, and inside on a shiny, silver plate was spaghetti and mixed vegetables with garlic bread, and on a smaller silver plate was a salad with lots of tomatoes and cucumbers. They also gave me blueberry pie, which was not my favorite, so I gave that one to my mom.

"I ate too much," I told my mom when I was finished. "They gave me too much food."

"They did give you a lot of food," said my mom. "You did not have to eat it all."

I was about to say something when the front desk speaker's announcement came on. "The hospital will be closing in five minutes. Visiting hours are over. We will reopen tomorrow at 8:00 a.m."

"Well, I guess I better go home," said my mom as she stood up and walked to the door. "See you tomorrow, sweetheart."

"Bye, Mom. I love you."

"I love you too, sweetheart."

Since visiting hours were over, I decided to call my friends Melanie and Melody. I couldn't wait to tell them the good news.

"Hi, Melody and Melanie," I said excitedly. "What's up? You are not going to believe the day I had today."

"Really! You had an exciting day at the hospital?" asked Melody. "Oh, hold on, Cynthia. I am going to put you on the speakerphone so Melanie can talk too."

I only heard the sound of footsteps stomping away from the phone to find Melanie. Melody must have been wearing those clunky sandals she always wears.

"It's Cynthia," said Melody. "She has some exciting news to tell us."

I heard something drop onto the floor. "What? What happened?" Melanie shrieked.

"Hi, Cynthia. I can't wait to hear about your day," said Melanie. "We have been missing you at school. Sorry, we have not been able to come and visit you, but our car is in the shop. We have been riding the bus for a couple of weeks now. We don't really enjoy—"

Melody interrupted her sister, "Can you please be quiet? Our BFF wants to tell us something exciting."

"All right, I am done, sis," said Melanie. "I will be quiet. It's just we haven't seen Cynthia in a while, and I had a lot more that I wanted to say. I will tell her the rest later."

"It better be a good story," said Melody. "We could really use some excitement around here."

"Oh, it is definitely a good story, Melody," I said.

"Go on. Tell us," Melanie and Melody said together. "We are dying to hear it."

"Okay, I was enjoying my sandwich while watching television; then, I suddenly heard a knock on my door. I asked who it was, and the person behind the door said, 'Jason.'"

"Wow!" said Melanie in shock. "He actually came to visit you?"

"Is he as cute close up as he is far away?" Melody teased.

"He is cute no matter what, and he also has a sweet side to him that I like."

"Aw, Cynthia is in love," said Melody and Melanie together. "She has found her amore."

"Hey guys, stop that; you are making me blush," I said. "Oh, I almost forgot to mention, he was about to give me a gift, and my mom walked in on us. It was really embarrassing; she started going on about how I was crushing on him. Jason and I were blushing like crazy."

"What did he buy you?" Melanie and Melody asked at the same time.

My best friends were getting impatient with me, but I still had a lot to say to them.

"After my mom left, he gave me a pink box with a sparkly pink ribbon, and inside was the most beautiful pink and opal bracelet with a dangling butterfly charm."

"Aw, how sweet," said Melanie. "He knows your favorite color."

"Yeah," I said in a soft, dreamy voice. "He said that he remembered my outfit from my first day of school, which was also pink, so that's how he knew pink was my favorite color."

"Did he give you a good night hug or kiss?" Melody asked curiously.

"No, I was hoping he would give me a hug or ask me out, but he did neither," I said. "I told him about me missing next week's game, so he said that he might record it for me. Then I told him we could watch it together at a later date. Maybe that will be our first date, but he is still with Brittany, so that will probably not happen."

"Oh, did you hear Brittany got suspended for what she did to you?" Melanie asked.

"Oh, really," I said as I was becoming suspicious. "Jason did not tell me that little bit of information. Maybe he did not know about it."

"Oh, he knew, Cynthia," said Melody. She repeated her phrase again. "Oh, he knew."

"Thank you so much, girls, for the info. I am going to hit the sack. I had enough excitement for one day. Good night, girls!"

"Good night," said Melanie and Melody.

I hung up the phone, laid down, and went right to sleep.

CHAPTER FOUR

Today, December 11, is the first day in two months that I have been able to walk around without my wheelchair. I felt so free like my life was becoming normal again. I know that I am not 100 percent better, but it feels so great to be up and walking around. My mom was holding my hand while I walked down the hall, and I suddenly let out an excited scream. It wasn't a really loud scream, but more of a shriek. I could tell that it bothered my mom a little bit since she jumped, but I thought it was funny. I was just too excited not to let my scream come out.

"You are doing great, honey," said my mom. "Keep on going. I believe you can do it. Just try not to scare me again, all right?"

"Well, I can't make any promises." My mom and I laughed so hard that we almost fell over.

I was beginning to become really tired as I reached the end of the hall. I wish I had more energy, but I think all of my energy went into trying to hold myself up when my mom and I were laughing so hard.

"Are you ready to go back to your room now?" My mom could tell that I was tired; she could see it in my eyes.

"Yes. I am tired, so ready to take a nap. Some sleep would feel really good right now." Even though I knew I wouldn't be able to sleep, I am just so excited that I am able to walk again. I will try to sleep, though; it just might take me a while.

"Okay, let's go," said my mom.

Only I wouldn't get to sleep as I planned. As soon as I got half-way to my room, I heard someone running really fast behind me and calling my name.

"Cynthia! Cynthia! Wait up! I have something to show you."

I swirled around slowly, almost like I was a dancer. I could not believe who I saw. It was Jason. My heart was pounding rapidly from walking, and plus, I was excited to see him. I looked into his eyes, and I could tell he was exhausted from chasing after me. I wanted to laugh, but I tried not to. I did not want Jason to think I was laughing at him. I just never thought a guy would chase after me as he did. I was getting really tired from standing, but I still had a little bit of energy left to talk to him. By the way, he came all the way down here to see me; I should at least say something to him.

"Hey Jason, long time, no see. What do you want to show me?"

"I have the last football game of your freshman year that you did not get a chance to see," said Jason. "I told you I would bring it the next time I came to visit."

"Awesome! It took you forever to bring it." I teased him as I giggled and touched Jason's shoulder. "I still want to see it."

"Do you have a DVD player in your room?" Jason asked.

"Yes, I do. It is underneath the television. You will have to use a stool to reach it because it is very high on the wall."

"Okay, I will race you to your room," said Jason.

"Hey, that's not fair," I told him. "You are healthier than I am."

I started walking faster, trying to keep up with Jason while pulling my mom behind me.

"Honey, you don't have to race him," said my mom. "I think he is just teasing you."

"I know, Mom, but I really want to see this game," I told her. "It's the last game of my freshman year."

I finally reached my door, and Jason said jokingly, "You're finally here. What took you so long?"

"Hey, quit teasing me, Jason," I giggled.

Both of us started laughing so hard that we both became teary-eyed, and we couldn't pronounce our words correctly.

Jason grabbed the stool that was in the bathroom and placed it under the television. "This is a nice little room you got here, Cynthia," said Jason as he stepped upon the stool to plug in the DVD player.

"Yes. It is nice, but it's not the same as my room at home," I replied.

Jason was just tall enough that he could reach the DVD player. There was a long cord hanging down the side of the DVD player. Jason grabbed the cord and plugged it into the socket that was on the wall behind the television.

"You sure got a tiny space here for your electronics," said Jason. "Everything is snug tightly on this wall. I hope it works. I had trouble getting my hand behind the television because everything here is tightly organized."

The light came on, and the DVD player started to work.

"The DVD player is working correctly, my lady," said Jason as if he were a royal prince from a faraway land.

"Yay!" I yelled as I giggled at Jason. He was so cute and funny at the same time.

I stood there looking at Jason, trying to picture him wearing a prince uniform with padded shoulders and a sash crossing over his right shoulder. He wasn't wearing a crown in my dream, but his blonde strands laid perfectly on his head. I thought he looked very handsome. Well, he always looks handsome to me, no matter what outfit he wears. Then I stood there picturing myself in a ball gown with my hair pinned in a bun. The Jason in my daydream started to bow down to me when his eyes saw me entering the ballroom. I felt like a real princess. As he was straightening up, he looked into my eyes, and he held out his hand. Then, out of the blue, my daydream was interrupted when I heard this loud and annoying static noise in the background. I couldn't figure out what the noise was. Or where it was coming from. Sadly, my daydream bubble popped and disappeared.

It was the old television set. Jason turned on the television to open the disc player, but he forgot to change the channel so the picture would come in clear instead of fuzzy. I placed my hands over my ears to protect them from the loud noise. I watched Jason step down the stool, one step at a time, and walk to the table in the corner of the room. He picked up the disk and walked back up the stool. As Jason stepped back up the stool, the DVD player's disc reader closed up.

"Oh, you've got to be kiddin' me," said Jason.

We both started laughing so hard that Jason almost fell off the stool. Poor Jason, he is having so much trouble with the DVD player. I busted out laughing again; it was just too funny.

"You better be careful, Jason. You might end up in here like me."

Jason opened the disk reader, placed the compact disk in the DVD player again, and changed the channel on the television. My mom sat in the chair by the table, and Jason came over to sit next to me on my bed. The disc reader closed, and it started playing the football game.

The game started off showing the cheerleaders standing in two rows shaking their pompoms in the air. A couple of the cheerleaders in the squad jumped up and did a split in the air. The others hollered and raised one arm with their index finger pointing up in the air. Then the cameraman focused his attention on the coach. The coach and staff held up a sign that read, "Go Bluesville Angels." The crowd was cheering as they knew the game was about to start. In just a few short moments, the audience stood up in the bleachers. Another cameraman ran to the side entrance to capture the exciting moment of the team's entrance. "Here they come," an announcer yelled in excitement. "This is going to be an exciting game for the Bluesville Angels." The cameraman near the entrance backed up to make room for the team. Coming around the corner was the football team running toward the banner. Jason, who was in the lead, led his team through the banner. The cameraman that was standing by the coach zoomed in to capture a close up of Jason's face. As Jason and his team went through, the banner ripped apart.

"There is my friend, Jason. You look so handsome in your football uniform," I said out loud without even thinking. I was so embarrassed; my face was totally red. I can't believe I just said that in front of him. I must have been out of my mind. Normally, I don't express my feelings about a guy out loud because doing so is so out of my comfort zone.

Maybe I am not as shy as I thought. Or maybe it was just the pain medication making me talk like this about my crush.

However, he did look really handsome, but I still never thought in a million years that I would say something like that in front of Jason and my mom. I looked at Jason, who was sitting next to me, then I glanced back at my mom. They were both so focused on the game that I don't think they heard me say a thing. Which was a good thing, I thought. Or was it? I mean, I finally said how I felt about a guy out loud, and no one in the room heard me. I looked at both of them again to see if I got a reaction from one of them. Nope, no reaction from Jason or my mom. So, I just shrugged my shoulders and continued to watch the game.

As I was watching the game, I heard Jason's phone beep on the bed. He must have gotten a text message from someone. I looked at Jason. Jason was so focused in the game that he didn't hear it. I was getting extremely curious about who was sending him a text message. So, I moved closer to his phone and noticed that the message was wide open and visible for me to see. The text read:

Hi sweetie. Where are you?
Love, Brittany

CHAPTER FIVE

I could not believe how fast this year went, and it was already Christmas time. I spent two months in the hospital, and I was finally being released today. You are probably wondering if I failed the first semester of my freshman year. I passed, thankfully, for my mom, who brought me my homework assignments to the hospital each day. If it weren't for my mom, I would have had to repeat the first semester of my freshman year again in the summer.

I have not seen Jason since the night I told him he was hot. I thought he did not hear me say it, but maybe he did because he has been avoiding me ever since. I sent him a text telling him about my last day in the hospital, but he hasn't replied back. Maybe he doesn't like me anymore. Or maybe he does like me? I am so confused. I keep receiving mixed signals from him, but maybe he is undecided on who he wants to date. I know that friendships can change over the years, and plus, he is not obligated to come here. I am not his girlfriend, but it was like really great to see him. Just somewhere deep inside my heart, I was still hoping that he would show up.

I was sitting on my chair, waiting for my mom to get the release papers. I was feeling restless, and I was also stiff from sitting in the same position for so long. So I got up to stretch my arms and walked over to the other side of my bed. I laid down on my back and thought about how much fun I had in this room with Jason. So many memories and our relationship may never be the same as it was here. Jason is going to be a junior, and I am going to be a year behind him. Then, I thought, maybe I can take part of my sophomore year in the summer and be a junior in the following spring with him. And then finish junior year that summer. But, I have one question to ask myself. Do I really want to rush my high school years for a boy?

I sat up on the edge of my bed and stretched out my hand to grab my cell phone on the table that was right next to me. I selected the message box and sent Jason a text:

> I am being released from the hospital today.
> Sorry you couldn't be here. I hope to see you soon.

I waited for about thirty minutes, and I still got no reply back from him.

I was looking at my phone, and my mom walked in and said, "Are you ready to leave, sweetie? I have all of the paperwork filled out; they just need you to sign a few documents."

"Really?" I said with excitement. "That's all I need to do, and I will be out of here?"

"Yes, since you are being released from the hospital today," said my mom. "To celebrate this wonderful occasion, how about we go get some ice cream?"

I could not believe that we were going to get some ice cream. I have not had some for ages. "Mom, that sounds great. I have to get a few things, and then I will be ready."

As I was packing up my belongings, I started to think about my health. I am so relieved that my bones are healed, and I can be my normal self again. I was glad that I was able to get up and walk around. It was no fun being in a wheelchair, but being in it made me think about how fortunate I am to be able to walk.

I picked up my phone, brush, lipstick, and my present from Jason. Then I stopped to look in the corner of my room to see if I left anything there. That part of my room was dark. My light bulb went out a couple of weeks ago, and it has been dark there ever since. All I could see was the shape of the coat rack. But as I walked closer, I noticed that something was there. It was a jacket, but it wasn't mine. I picked up the jacket and took it to a place where I had light. It was Jason's blue sports jacket. I could not believe that I did not see this before. I was extremely shocked. Why would Jason leave his number twenty-six jacket here? I placed his jacket on my chair and searched through his pockets. I did not find anything but a small package.

I took the small box out of his jacket pocket and quickly placed it on the table. Is this for Brittany or me? I automatically thought it was for Brittany since she is Jason's girlfriend. So, I decided to put it back into his coat pocket. Perhaps I should send a text to Jason to tell him that he left his jacket here by accident. I wouldn't want him to worry about a gift that was meant for someone else. But then I thought maybe he did leave it here deliberately. He did surprise me with a bracelet when he came to visit me that one day. Maybe it was just another surprise from him. I took out the present and looked at it again. Well, the box was pink, which was my favorite color. Then, all of a sudden, I remembered that Brittany only likes purple. So, it couldn't possibly be for Brittany.

I untied the pink ribbon and opened the lid of the box. It was the cutest thing I have ever seen. Inside was a little pink football charm with the number twenty-six engraved on the front. *Jason is so sweet*, I thought as I smiled happily. I am going to have to thank him the next time I see him.

I looked around the room one more time, thinking of the great memories I had in here with Jason. We had such a good time together. I am going to miss spending time with him. But even with the good memories, I was so eager to get out of here.

I opened the door, and my mom asked, "Are you ready to go?"

"Yes, I sure am."

My mom and I walked all the way down to the end of the hall.

We approached the elevator, and I pressed number one, and it glowed like a candle. I dislike elevators so much because I am afraid that the elevator will stop working when I am in it, and I will not be able to get out.

It seemed like I was in the elevator forever. The only thing that kept me from being terrified was that my mom was in there with me. My mom and I were both quiet the whole time, and the only sound we could hear was the soft jazz that was playing in the speakers. Then, the elevator bumped the side wall coming down, and my mom and I held onto the side wall till it straightened out and hit the first floor. The bump wasn't bad, but it sure did scare me a little. From looking at the elevator, it didn't appear old, but from the way it landed, it felt ancient. The number-one button's glow went out, and the doors reopened.

"We have one more thing to do before we leave," said my mom as she walked out of the elevator, pointed her index finger up in the air, and turned around to look at me.

I can't believe my mom. She just walked out of the elevator so calm, as if nothing happened. While I, on the other hand, was still standing in the elevator with my knees trembling and my heart beating rapidly. I wish I could be more calm like my mom when these types of things occur in life. I guess it just comes with the territory of being a news reporter.

My mom watched me as I quickly walked out of the elevator. "I have to take you to the front desk so that you can sign the departure papers."

I still had the departure papers to sign. It seemed like everything was keeping me from leaving this place. From the memories of Jason to the elevator almost breaking down. I felt like I was stuck here and unable to leave—kind of like a lion who is trapped in a cage all day and can't get out.

I walked to the front desk, and the lady gave me some papers to sign. I signed and dated them all and gave them back to her. I anxiously awaited as she checked each document.

"Okay," said the lady behind the desk. "You are all set to go, Ms. Adams."

"Thank you," I replied with a sigh of relief that I was almost out of here.

I looked up at the lady after I said thank you. She was about five-foot-three with beautiful, long red hair. Her eyes were hazel, and her skin was white as the clouds in the sky. I smiled at her, and she smiled back.

I turned around to see my mom standing outside by the doorway. The sun was shining brightly, and the air appeared to be windy. I could tell it was windy by my mom's hair blowing to the side. I ran toward the front entrance and exited the sliding doors.

"Oh, it feels so great out here," I said excitedly. "It must be sixty-five degrees outside. I have not been able to enjoy weather like this for two months." Then I turned toward my mom and asked, "Mom, are we still going to get some ice cream, as you suggested earlier?"

"Yes, we are," said my mom as she took out a cold lime soda from her purse and handed it to me. "Do you want to go to Blue Freeze? I know it is your favorite."

I nodded and smiled at her.

It is funny that everything is called "Blue" something or other around here. I guess you can call our town the blue town. Anyway, Blue Freeze is the hottest hangout for high school and college students. Before I went to the hospital, Melody, Melanie, Stanley, and I used to go there every Friday after school. This place has every flavor possible. If you want it, they probably have it. One time, my friends and I went there, and they had this really weird dessert. It was called Captain Blue's Shark Attack. The restaurant made this dessert to show what happens to the small fish after a shark has attacked. The base was blue jelly mixed with blueberry ice cream. Above the base, there was an assortment of fish-like candies layered on top of the water. Some of the candies were broken in half to make the fish look like they have been eaten by a shark. Those same candies were arranged differently in the blue base to give the customers the impression that the fish were floating on top of the water. They did a good job at displaying this effect, but it made the dessert look too realistic. It made me feel sorry for the fish, so I decided not to order one. Melody and Melanie looked at it after I did, and they decided not to order it either. We all looked at each other and curled up our lips in disgust. It was just too gross for us.

When our ice cream arrived at our table, we all started giggling when we found out that Stanley ordered a Captain Blue's Shark Attack. The server placed our ice cream on our table one at a time—first one chocolate, next raspberry, then strawberry. But when she placed the Captain Blue's Shark Attack on the table, none of us could even look at Stanley's ice cream. We were turning our heads, making faces, and staring at Stanley.

When he caught us staring at him, he just looked at us and said, "What?" and continued eating.

Melanie, her sister, and I looked at each other and whispered, "Eww, gross."

I smiled as I remembered that Stanley really enjoyed eating that dessert that night. He didn't care if it looked gross or not; he still wanted to eat it. That's why I like Stanley; he is open to trying new things.

My mom and I walked across the parking lot to search for our car. She had this strange, bewildered look on her face.

"You know what, honey?" my mom said as she searched the parking lot. "I can't seem to remember where I parked the car this morning."

"Did you park it on the right side of the hospital?" I told her. "That's usually where you park."

"I think you are right, sweetie. Thanks for keeping your mom straight."

Even when my grandma was here, my mom parked in the same spot. That parking spot must have our name written all over it.

Suddenly I started to laugh, and my mom asked, "What is so funny?"

"Nothing," I told my mom as I kept moving my mouth in different ways to keep from smiling. I didn't want my mom to think I was laughing at her, even though I was. But I think she knew. So, every few minutes, my mom would give me a strange facial expression. Each look of hers was funnier than the one before. I took a sip of my lime soda; then I looked at my mom again. The last look she gave me was the funniest. I couldn't hold my laugh in any longer, so I just exploded. The lime soda in my mouth flew out everywhere. I mean, ubiquitously. It was so embarrassing, but it made my mom crack up.

We continued walking to the right side of the hospital. I passed a blue car, then a pink and green car, which reminded me of a watermelon. Seeing those two colors together made me have a craving for watermelon. Maybe I could order a couple of scoops of watermelon ice cream at Blue Freeze to satisfy my craving. But, as we walked further away from the pink and green car, my craving for a slice of juicy watermelon automatically disappeared.

Near the right side of the hospital, we passed two motorcycles, which were parked in between two big vans. It kind of reminded me of a van sandwich with those small motorcycles stuck in between two gigantic vans. However, I was more interested in the motorcycles. I have never ridden one, but I always wanted to. I wonder whom those motorcycles belong to. But since I am leaving, I guess I will never find out who owns them.

We walked from the parking lot to a small sidewalk. By the sidewalk was a small garden with many bright red roses, white lilies, and pink tulips. I wish I had brought my camera with me so that I could take pictures of these pretty flowers.

"Mom, I see our car up ahead."

I walked as fast as I could to get to the car, even though my energy is not like it used to be. Finally, I reached my mom's purple car, opened the door, and hopped in the back seat.

My mom was close to approaching the car when I suddenly heard a beep coming from my phone. At that same moment, my mom opened the front car door, sat down, put on her seat belt, and said, "You must be really excited to get some ice cream."

"Yes, I am," I told her while staring at my phone.

I opened the message, and it was from Jason. I was shocked to hear from him. I didn't think he would text me back.

I was becoming so nervous. Why am I feeling this way? I want to read it, but I am afraid that the message will be something about Brittany. But I am so curious. I have to read it; it might be important.

> Sorry, I could not be there. I had football practice all day, and my coach would not let me leave.

My cell phone beeped again, and the message box popped up.

> I have nothing to do right now. Do you want to meet somewhere in about fifteen to twenty minutes?

I sent a text back to Jason.

> My mom and I are going to Blue Freeze. You are welcome to come if you want.

My mom turned around from the front seat and asked, "Who are you talking to?"

"It is Jason, Mom," I told her. "I invited him to come to Blue Freeze with us to celebrate getting out of the hospital. He has not sent me a reply to tell me that he is coming yet."

Just after I said that Jason sent me a reply back:

> Sure, that sounds like fun. I love ice cream.
> I will see you in about twenty minutes.

"He is coming, Mom," I said as I started to giggle and squeal.

CHAPTER SIX

Blue Freeze is the hot spot of our small town. The place where everyone comes to get the most unique ice cream. As I entered the building, I was rather shocked about how many people showed up. The people that showed up were mostly teenage girls on dates with their boyfriends. This place is always crowded, but today it was more packed than usual, like it was Valentine's Day or something.

In the middle of the room is an aisle where you stand to place your order. The ordering aisle divides the room right down the middle. On each side of the aisles are blue, round tables scattered around with at least two chairs positioned at each table.

I was waiting for my mom to park the car, and all of a sudden, Brittany shows up with another boy. I thought this boy might have gone to our school, but his face was so unfamiliar to me. I looked at Brittany with her curled hair dangling over her shoulders. She was wearing bright red lipstick that matched the red dots of her white polka-dotted dress. After I looked at her hair and her dress, I looked down at her shoes. They were bright, shiny red heels. She stopped talking to her friend and looked at me with a surprised stare. I guess she was shocked to see me out of the hospital.

"Oh my goodness . . . umm . . . umm. I can't seem to remember your name," she says while trying to pretend that she doesn't recognize me. "It has been a long time since I have seen you."

"Oh, really, Brittany? It has not been that long. Let me refresh your memory, Brittany. My name is Cynthia Adams, and I am the one you put in the hospital two months ago."

"Oh yeah, I remember you," she said with a smirk on her face.

"So . . . Brittany. May I ask, who is your friend?" I said curiously. "What are you guys doing here?"

"Well . . . this is Steve Langley, and we are on a date." Brittany grabbed Steve's arm and said, "Isn't he like, so cute?"

I thought this is weird. I thought Brittany was dating Jason, but I was so curious that I decided to ask her anyway, without thinking of the consequences. She has already sent me to the hospital. What else could she do that would be worse than that?

"Brittany, I thought you were dating, Jason," I said. "How could—"

Steve interrupted with an angry expression on his face. "Who is Jason? You told me you were not dating anyone."

"Well, Steve . . . I am dating Jason, but he bailed on me. He made some lame excuse that he was going to see his grandma or something like that," Brittany replied as she rolled her eyes and fluffed her hair.

I was thinking in my head, why doesn't Jason tell Brittany the truth? He is coming to see me after all . . . that's what he told me. What is he so afraid of?

Brittany interrupts my thought with her phony, sweet attitude. "Come on, Steve. Let's go somewhere else more romantic than this ice cream place."

"Well, it was so nice seeing you again, Brittany. Tell Jason I said hi."

"Okay, sure. Like that is so going to happen," Brittany said in a sarcastic voice as she grabbed Steve's hand to signal to him that she was ready to leave.

As she got closer to the exit, she turned her head around and glared at me for a few seconds. Those few seconds were horrifying. My face felt so hot . . . almost like I was breathing in smoke from a fire. Brittany turned back, facing the door, and let out a hysterically evil laugh as she walked out of the ice cream restaurant.

I couldn't believe her laughing at me like that, especially in front of Steve. I thought Steve would leave her after he found out that she was dating Jason, but he didn't. He just stood there as she finished her conversation with me. If you could call what we did a conversation.

As I was trying to figure out what to make of our conversation, my mom came in with a concerned expression on her face.

"Honey, I just saw Brittany leave. Are you okay?"

"I am fine, Mom. Brittany is just trying to ruin my life. I am trying not to let her actions bother me."

"That's good, honey. I like your attitude about this situation, but you still look upset to me. Do you want to talk about it?"

"Sure, I guess if you want to, but there is not much to talk about. She just came in here flirting with Steve while at the same time making my life more miserable. As usual."

My mom had a confused expression on her face. "Who is Steve? I thought she was dating, umm . . . what's his name? The guy you have a crush on."

"Mom! Don't be so loud; everyone can hear you," I whispered as my cheeks glowed a deeper red. I looked nervously around the room to see if anyone heard what my mom said. Then my mom joined me, and we noticed a couple of people staring at us.

"Oh, sorry, dear," said my mom. "Please, go on."

"Brittany is still dating Jason, but she got a last-minute date replacement because Jason gave her an excuse," I explained.

"What do you mean by 'excuse'?"

"He told her he was going to visit his grandma instead of telling her the truth that he was actually coming to meet me at Blue Freeze," I said.

"Honey, do you think you should really be seeing this guy? I mean, can you really trust him? He has already lied to Brittany. Do you think he might be lying to you?"

My mom was asking too many questions that I thought my head was going to explode. I tried to breathe calmly to help me focus on the answers to her questions, but it didn't help. I was just too overwhelmed. Of course, I do want to see Jason, and I want to trust him. I want to believe that he is telling the truth. But how will I be able to trust him if he has already lied to Brittany?

The more I thought this over, the more overwhelmed I became. So, I just stuck to what I believed was right. "No, he would never lie to me."

I was so frustrated, to calm down I just let my eyes wander. I focused my attention on a young couple kissing in the corner of the room. I thought it was so romantic. I hope that one day I will be able to kiss a guy like that. Then I moved my eyes away from the couple to a nearby window. Through the window, I spotted Jason walking toward the entrance of the ice cream shop. He walked so cool like he had no care in the world. I got out of my little daydream and went right back into reality.

"See, Mom, here is Jason right now," I exclaimed as I pointed at Jason. "He did not lie to me."

"Okay, dear," said my mom. "Have fun."

"You're not going to join us?" I asked.

"No, I have a list of errands to get done. Plus, I have to go across the street to buy something to cook for dinner tonight. You two have fun."

"We will; bye, Mom. See you in a couple of hours," I told her as she walked out the door.

Jason walked through the door with his hair blowing from the wind.

"Hello, Cynthia. Sorry, I am late. I had to go see my grandma to see if she needed anything," Jason replied. "She lives alone, so I go and check on her every day."

"That's so sweet of you, Jason," I said.

I knew it; he was telling the truth. I wish I would have trusted my intuition sooner. Suddenly the dreadful conversation that I had with Brittany just popped into my mind. Of all the times for it to come up—when I am trying to get to know Jason better. What am I going to say to Jason about seeing Brittany with another guy? What will he say? Will he be upset if I tell him? Should I even tell him?

"Yeah, I like being with her; she teaches me a lot," said Jason. "Are you okay, Cynthia? You look a little bummed."

"Yeah, I am fine. Well, not really. Your girlfriend came in here with another man. I guess I shouldn't have brought it up, but it has been on my mind since it happened."

"Oh, really? That is so like Brittany. She can't seem to wait a day for me, so she just goes out with some random dude she meets who knows where. Cynthia, don't let her bother you; it is just her nature. She is not a patient girl." Jason starts to laugh. "Oh, anyway, enough about Brittany. Would you like to get a bite to eat?"

"Sure," I said. I can't believe I am actually out with Jason. This is like a dream come true for me.

Jason and I walked up to the counter to look at the different kinds of ice cream they had available. This place has favorites like chocolate, vanilla, strawberry, and black raspberry, but they are also known for their rare flavors, which come out on Valentine's Day, Easter, Halloween, and Christmas. After we looked at the flavors, we got back in line. The line was about halfway to the door.

While waiting for our turn to order, I noticed that one of the guys behind the counter was really nervous. I couldn't see what he looked like from being so far away from the counter, but all I could see was his job performance. He kept messing up orders and dropping money that the customers gave him. Every time he messed up, one of his co-workers would yell at him. I felt so sorry for him; he was doing the best he could. I can't imagine the pressure he has to exceed in his job.

After about ten minutes of waiting, it was finally time for Jason and me to order. We stepped up to the register, and the nervous guy that I noticed earlier started to wait on us.

"Hi . . . umm . . . welcome . . . to umm . . . Blue Freeze. Umm . . . may . . . . umm . . . take your order?"

As I got a closer look at him, I got a glimpse of his name tag. His name was Tyler. After I found out his name, I looked down at his left hand and noticed it was shaking terribly. Poor guy; he is so nervous. I wanted to say something to him to make him feel less anxious, but I didn't want the guy to become more panicky.

"I would like a couple of scoops of black raspberry in a cup," I said with a smile. Then Tyler glanced at Jason without saying a word.

"I want a lime sorbet," said Jason as he put his hand in his right pocket.

"Do you . . . um . . . want your ice cream . . . um . . . in a cup?"

"Sure, that's fine," said Jason as he started searching his pocket for his wallet.

It took him forever to punch in our order. When he was finally done, I grabbed both of our ice cream cups and went to search for a table while Jason paid the bill. I thought it was nice that he offered to pay the bill; he is such a gentleman. I found an empty table among the crowd that was by a window on the right side of the room. I placed our ice cream cups on the round table, and I looked at the stool. The stool was very cute. It had a vanilla ice cream cone in the center, and the cushion was blue. I sat down on my ice cream stool and started to eat my raspberry ice cream.

Meanwhile, when Jason was paying the bill, he noticed a small tray of ice cream cone charms sitting next to the register. Since he remembered that pink was Cynthia's favorite color, he bought her one to add to her collection.

Without telling Cynthia, Jason walked out of the ice cream shop and went out to his car. He unlocked his car with his remote key and opened the trunk door. Inside, he had his tools, car jack included, and some sports magazines stacked on the left side of the trunk.

Jason was hoping he would find a box in his car that would fit her charm. He wasn't prepared this time to find a present like he was the last time; it was just a last-minute find. On the right, lying by itself, was a bright pink colored box. It was small indeed, but it was just the perfect size for Cynthia's charm. Jason smiled and was relieved that he had an extra one. He knew he didn't have time to go to the store to buy another box since Cynthia was in there waiting for him. So, Jason picked up the box and gently placed the charm inside. Jason pushed the trunk down, locked his car, and put the present in his pocket. He walked around to the front of his car, stepped onto the sidewalk, and went back inside the ice cream shop.

Cynthia was still eating her ice cream when Jason sat in the seat right across from her.

"What took you so long?" I said as I took another bite of my ice cream. "Your sorbet is melting."

"Sorry about that," said Jason. "I had to do an errand." Jason picked up his spoon and took a bite of his half-melted sorbet. "How does it feel to be out of the hospital?"

"Jason, it feels so great to be out of there. I would get so lonely at night. I would hear all sorts of things that would keep me awake."

"I am so glad that you are out of there, too. I am so sorry that Brittany did that to you . . . she had no right to do so."

"I know, but that is over and done with now."

While I was finishing my ice cream, I started thinking about the dance—The Beyond the Sea Dance that was coming up next year in March.

As I took my last bite, I said, "So . . . the Beyond the Sea Dance is coming up. Who is going to be your date?"

"Well, gosh . . . I actually had not thought about it," said Jason. "I would really like to take you, Cynthia, to the dance, but Brittany probably would not allow it since we are together."

"Really? You would?" I said in shock. It was really nice to hear that he wanted to take me to the dance. I knew he couldn't take me, though, since he was so committed to his relationship with Brittany. But on the other hand, Brittany wasn't. I felt like Brittany was cheating on Jason. Thinking about this reminded me of Brittany being on a date with Steve. How come Brittany can go out with other people, but he can't? It just doesn't seem fair to him.

"Jason, I think you should be allowed to take anyone you want to the dance without asking Brittany for permission. I mean, she is already out on a date with another guy right now because she couldn't go with you. So, why can't you ask out other girls?"

"I know. I completely understand what you are saying. I am going to wait till January or February to ask a girl to the dance."

"Oh, okay," I said while thinking about his reaction. He didn't seem to be too upset about Brittany being with another guy. He was calm and relaxed and not the least bit jealous. On the other hand,

Brittany gets extremely jealous when other girls make eye contact with him. Thinking about all of this was starting to give me a headache, so I decided to change the subject. "What are you going to do for Christmas, Jason?"

"I am going to Brittany's parents house to hang out for the holidays. Her parents are the best cooks ever. They make the best sweet potato casserole I have ever tasted. I can't wait to eat their food. I am getting hungry just thinking about it."

"Wow! Jason, that sounds like a lot of fun. I hope you have a good time."

I felt a little bummed that he was spending Christmas with Brittany, but as long as he had fun, I was okay with it.

"Cynthia, what are your plans for Christmas?"

"My brother Brian and sister Ashley are coming home from college to celebrate Christmas with us. I don't get to see them much because they both live in another state for school."

"I can't wait for my college years to start. I want to apply to Blue State University to work on my pre-med degree, then I will play football in the fall," said Jason. "I have wanted to be a doctor since I was about five years old."

"Wow! Jason, it sounds like you have your life all planned out for you. I still have a couple of years before I decide what to do next after high school. Well, I better get going; my mom is waiting out in the car for me. I really enjoyed this conversation we had today."

"So did I," said Jason.

Jason and I stood up, pushed in our chairs, and we grabbed our empty ice cream cups to throw out. Jason walked ahead of me while I followed him. I still couldn't believe that I was actually at Blue Freeze and not in my hospital room. I had to pinch my arm a few times to see if being at Blue Freeze was actually a dream or if it was really happening.

On our way out, Jason and I walked past many tables of teenagers hanging out, and then I saw the same couple kissing in the corner of the room. They are still here? I can't believe they are still kissing. They must really love each other.

Anyway, before you get to the cash register, there is a small hall-way section that has a counter where you can get extra napkins, spoons, and toppings. We stopped there and dropped our cups into the trash can. While standing there, apparently Jason received a text message from someone, so I decided to walk ahead of him to the door. While I stood by the door, I placed my hand on the glass and looked out the window. I didn't see much through the window except for a few cars driving by. I twirled around to look at Jason. He was sending his reply, and when he was done, he glanced up at me. He was surprised to see that I was still here and by the door. I guess he thought I had left already. Jason quickly ran to the entrance and opened the door for me.

Aw, he is such a gentleman.

As he was opening the door for me, the feelings that I had for him returned. I don't know why I didn't feel this way earlier. I guess I felt so comfortable talking to him like a friend that I forgot he was the most popular guy in school. Thinking about his popularity status made me remember that I had his jacket in my mom's car.

"Oh, Jason, I forgot to tell you that I have your jacket in the car. You left it at the hospital the last time you came."

"Thanks, Cynthia," said Jason as he secretly slipped a pink box inside Cynthia's side pocket of her jacket. "I was wondering where I left it."

Jason walked with me to my mom's car. I handed him his sports jacket, and we said our goodbyes. I stood by my mom's car as I watched him get into his Mustang and drive off.

I opened the car door and sat down. I felt something weird and lumpy in the side pocket of my jacket. I did not remember putting anything in my pockets today. I took a look inside, and there was a surprise pink box. I grabbed the package from out of my pocket and placed it on my lap. That sneaky Jason. I opened it up, and inside was the most beautiful ice cream charm I have ever seen.

CHAPTER SEVEN

Well, it is a holly, jolly Christmas, and the best time of the year, as the song says. This is my favorite time of year when you can spend quality time with your family and eat so much food that you can no longer eat anymore. Every year, my brother Brian and I eat so much food that we both can't move for the rest of the night. The image of us lying there stuffed sounds funny once you think about it for a moment.

It was Christmas Eve morning when I woke up to the sound of my family laughing downstairs. That's the one thing that I like about my family—we love to laugh and have a good time. I automatically sat up with my legs in an Indian style position while I focused my attention on my clock. I couldn't see the time clearly since my eyes were still a little bit blurry from just waking up. A couple of minutes later, I rubbed my eyes and looked at my clock once more. My eyes were so much clearer this time, and it was only nine. I think nine o'clock is way too early for people to be awake in the morning, especially at Christmas time. Since it was still early, I wrapped my pillow around my head and tried to go back to sleep.

About an hour later, I sat up again. I was just so excited to see my brother and sister that I couldn't go back to sleep. While still not awake, I got out of my bed and put on my festive red shirt, blue jeans, and red slippers. I usually don't wear many clothes that aren't the color pink, but since it was Christmas time, I made an exception. I walked halfway down the stairs to find my brother Brian and sister Ashley standing by the couch waiting for me. I was so excited to see them that I rushed down the rest of the stairs so fast that one of my slippers slid from underneath my foot, causing me to fall right on my bottom.

My brother Brian heard a loud thump and looked up at the stairway. "Be careful, little sis; you don't want to be in the hospital again."

I stood straight up, smiled, and walked over to my sister and brother.

Brian gave me a hug, and then my sister Ashley said, "How are you feeling, sis? I am so glad that you are out of the hospital. How was your first year at Bluesville High? Did you meet any cute guys?"

My sister was asking so many questions at once that I didn't know which one to answer first. I stood there for a few minutes, thinking about how I was feeling at the moment. Well, I was feeling good today until I fell on my bottom. The stair incident was the only thing I could consider talking about at that very moment. I looked at my sister with my eyebrows down and my eyes were looking off to the side. We began to laugh as my sister could tell that I was confused. I guess my sister finally realized that she asked me too many questions at once. So, my sister and I walked over to sit on the couch while my brother and dad helped mom in the kitchen.

"I am so glad to see you, sis. I am feeling great. Well, except for the pain in my bottom," I said as I started to laugh. "We have so much to talk about."

"Great! I want to hear about everything," said Ashley. "We haven't had a good chat in a while."

While I was having a conversation with my sister, my mother and father were cooking our Christmas Eve dinner. As my mom was waiting for the turkey to finish cooking, she began to lay out the sweet potatoes and green bean casserole on the counter. In about ten minutes, the turkey was done, and my mom grabbed her oven mitt, got the turkey out of the oven, and placed it on the counter next to the sweet potatoes and green beans.

As I was listening to my sister talk about her classes, I glanced across the room to see if dinner was ready. I didn't find out if dinner was ready, but what I noticed instead was what my brother was doing. He was making sure that Mom and Dad weren't looking, then he rubbed his hands together and started to peel off a piece of turkey. My jaw dropped in shock as I continued to watch him to see if he gets caught. Then my sister stopped talking and noticed that my mouth was wide open. She appeared confused as to why I was flabbergasted and staring off into the distance. Ashley looked across the room and saw my brother, and we both looked at each other and started laughing. My mom turned around to see what the laughter was about and saw my brother stealing a big bite of turkey.

"Hey, you!" yelled my mother. "Get out of my turkey, you bad boy."

"Hey, I almost had it, until my sisters caught me in the act," said Brian. "You guys always get me into trouble, but I don't care. I love you guys anyway."

"I got a piece, but nobody noticed me," said my father as he grabbed an apple from the fruit basket and took a bite out of it.

"No fair!" my brother exclaimed.

Then we all started to laugh again.

When we stopped laughing at my silly brother Brian, I continued my conversation with my sister Ashley.

"I had many unusual experiences at Bluesville High, some that I probably will never forget."

My sister's eyes started to sparkle with excitement. "Oh, sis. I am dying inside to hear all about your experiences. What would you like to tell me first?"

"Well, I got to see my friends Stanley, Melanie, and Melody again, and we ate lunch at the same table every day. My classes were okay, but the best class was algebra, where I met the cutest guy ever."

I stopped talking for a moment and looked at my parents

preparing dinner, hoping that the meal was almost ready. Ashley was impatient and very fascinated in hearing what I had to say. "Come on, continue; this is starting to get interesting. I want to hear all about this cute boy."

Inside, I really did not want to continue talking about Jason because once I start to mention his name, I probably would never hear the end of it. She will constantly tease me about him every time we see each other. So, I did not talk much about Jason but moved the focus of the conversation to his weird, mean, but popular girlfriend. I told my sister all of the mean things Brittany did to me after I looked at her boyfriend.

"That girl is so jealous of you," said Ashley. "She probably thinks you are going to steal her boyfriend away from her."

"That's what my friends say, but I don't believe it."

"So . . . how cute is this guy, anyway?" asked my sister as she rested her jaw on the palm of her hand. "You haven't spoken much about him."

So as I was about to open my mouth to speak about Jason, my mom interrupted and said, "Dinner is ready. Come and eat."

I was so thankful and relieved that my mom interrupted at that very moment, so I wouldn't have to talk about my crush. I know my sister was really excited to hear about Jason, but I just couldn't do it, well . . . not with my whole family listening. That would have been really embarrassing.

Everyone walked to the table and sat down to eat. The turkey, green bean casserole, salad, and sweet potatoes looked so delicious. Although, all I could think about was that I almost spilled the beans about Jason, him spending time with me, and the bracelet.

Later that night, after dinner, I looked out the window, and I saw white, fluffy pieces of snow falling from the sky. We are actually having a white Christmas after all. In the dark, I saw a young guy walking to a blue car that was parked in front of my neighbor's house down the street. Then I realized it must have been one of my neighbor's sons visiting their parents while on Christmas break.

Without further consideration of who the guy might be, I stepped out on the front porch and watched the snow fall and stick to the ground. I walked out in the yard without putting on my hat and coat and just let the snow fall on me. I looked at my mom's flower bushes, and they were all covered with snow. I was so happy that it was snowing that I started twirling around. The cold, shimmering white snow was in my hair and on my clothes. I even got some snow in my mouth. My body was getting so cold that I was starting to feel sick.

I walked up the steps and turned around to glance at the snow once more. As I turned to face the door, I saw a rectangular-shaped object sitting underneath the snow. I almost did not see it since most of the snow was covering it. I uncovered the snow from the box and picked it up. I wasn't sure who the package was for, but I decided to open the box anyway. I lifted the lid, and inside were two beautiful charms: a Christmas tree and a snowflake. Then, all of a sudden, I realized that the guy I saw walking to his car earlier must have been Jason. All of these thoughts flowed through my mind, but the one question stood out more than the others. Why didn't he ring our doorbell to tell me that he was here? I guess he didn't want to bother us at Christmas time. I would have loved to have seen him on Christmas. I can't believe I just missed him. I held my present tightly in my hand as I just stood there, staring at the snow.

"Has anyone seen Cynthia?" I heard my mom cry out while I was standing outside in the cold, icy snow. I would have answered her, but I just wanted to be alone for a few minutes.

"No, I haven't seen her," I heard my brother yell.

"I saw her go outside about ten minutes ago," I heard my sister Ashley tell my mother in the living room. "I don't know if she is still out there, but I will look." In the corner of my eye, I saw my sister walk to the window. She was about to pull back the curtain when I heard her speak again. "But she's probably upstairs. I know my sister; she wouldn't stay out in the cold too long." Ashley pulled back the curtain. "What? Mom, come look. She is just standing there. Is she okay?"

"I don't know, but I will find out," my mom said in her concerned voice. "I wish someone would have told me her whereabouts sooner before I became worried."

"Sorry, mom," said my sister. "I had no idea that she was still out there. She shouldn't be out there in the cold without a jacket."

My mom walked to the window and looked out at me. I was aware of everything going on, but I was still too upset to get out of the cold. I just froze there like a piece of ice waiting to melt. I heard my mom walk to the front door, and the door squeaked as it opened.

"Are you okay, honey? It is too cold to stand out here. Come back inside, Cynthia, before you catch a cold."

I walked back into the house as my brother Brian and sister Ashley were putting the tree together. As they heard the front door slam, they both stopped what they were doing and turned around to face me. From their worried expressions to their hands folded together gave me the impression that my siblings knew I was upset about something. They were right . . . my brother and sister know me way too well.

"What's wrong?" my brother and sister asked at the same time.

"Nothing . . . I am fine," I said with a fake smile as I walked quietly up the steps to my room. I placed my present from Jason on the table next to my bed and laid on my back. I started to stare at my beautiful pink ceiling fan when many of my tears fell gradually down my cheeks. How do my brother and sister always know that I am upset about something? Maybe they see it on my face? Or is it because they know me so well? I am very close to my brother and sister but talking about my crush is one thing that's hard for me to talk about. I am so upset. My tears started to fall down my face like raindrops falling out of a cloud. How could I have missed him? Thinking about how I missed Jason coming over only made me cry harder. I must really like or even love this guy if I keep crying over him.

I heard my family talking to each other downstairs.

"Is she all right?" I heard my brother saying.

"I don't know, Brian," said my sister. "She seems to be upset about something."

"Like what?" my brother asked with confusion.

"How should I know?" my sister said sarcastically.

"What is all of this commotion about?" my father said as he entered the living room.

"Our sister, Cynthia, is upset about something," said Ashley. "We don't know what is wrong. She seemed so happy earlier."

"Well . . . one of you should go upstairs and check on her, instead of asking each other what is wrong," said my father. "You will never know the answer unless you ask the one who has the troubles."

So I heard my mom say, "I will go upstairs and check on her."

As soon as I heard the sound of her footsteps coming up the stairs, I quickly sat up and dried my tears before she could see me. As she reached closer to my door, I saw that I left Jason's present out on the table for anyone to see. I didn't want my mom to see the gift that I received from Jason. That same gift was secretly given to me, which therefore caused me to be upset at Jason for not telling me he was here. I just didn't want my mom to know that I was crying about Jason, and I wasn't ready to talk to her about the gift he gave me.

I quickly jumped out of my bed to grab the present. Then I quickly ran to my dresser that was in front of my bed, opened the top sock drawer, and placed it in there. After that, I ran to the side of my bed and grabbed one of my fashion magazines that was lying on the floor, and jumped back onto my bed. I held my magazine in my hands, and I pretended to read it while I waited for my mom to come into my room.

In just a few short seconds, I heard a soft knock on my door. "Honey, may I come in and talk to you for a few minutes?"

"Sure, Mom. You can come in," I said as I continued looking at my magazine. "What would you like to talk about?"

"Well, sweetie . . . I would like to talk to you about why you are so sad on Christmas Eve. Did something happen earlier today that made you feel this way? You know you can talk to me about anything."

After she said that, I placed my magazine on my lap and I started to think. Do I really want to bring this up now? It is Christmas Eve and all, and plus, the whole family is here. I really should be downstairs with them getting ready for Christmas instead of crying in my room.

"Well . . . I do have something that is bothering me, but can we talk about it later when the whole family is not here? I don't want everyone to know about it, especially my sister; you know how she is, Mom."

My mom's eyes were wide open, and right then, she figured out that I was upset about a boy. I know that this shocking expression means boys because she gave that same look to my sister when she was having boy troubles.

My sister has always been obsessed with boys her whole life. She has always been popular since a young age. My sister was a cheerleader like Brittany, but she was nice to everybody she was around. She has dated guys since middle school, but she hasn't found her one true love. Ashley has always told me that she wants to one day find the man of her dreams, that one man she will spend the rest of her life with, and the one man that will love her for who she truly is. She doesn't want a man that loves her just because she is pretty or popular. My sister is pretty deep when it comes to love, and my mom is the same way. I guess I get that from them. Love is more than loving someone for their looks or popularity; it is about caring for one another through the good and the bad times. Love is what gets you through life. If we didn't have one another, life would be unbearable. My mother and sister have taught me a lot about love, and I learned it all from them.

"Okay, we can talk about this later," my mom told me. "Dry up your tears and come downstairs. We are about to put ornaments on the tree."

I nodded my head and said, "I will be down in a few minutes."

My mom walked out into the hallway and turned around to look at me once more. She grabbed and slowly pulled the door knob closed, and when the door was almost shut, a cheerful smile came upon her face. When she left the room, I grabbed a couple of tissues and started to wipe my eyes again. I got out of bed, placed my slippers back on my feet, and walked out into the hallway. As I reached closer to the stairs, I heard my family singing, "Deck the Halls." I slowly crept down the stairs as the song ended, and then I noticed my brother Brian singing solo as he was placing the angel on top of the tree.

After that, my brother noticed I was downstairs and said, "Hey, there's my little sis. We are glad you came downstairs to see us. Come and help us decorate the tree; it's a lot of fun."

I grabbed my favorite ornament: a miniature, sparkly pink high heel shoe, and placed it in the same spot where the light shines in from the window, which makes my shoe sparkle so much that it reminds me of a star, or maybe, in my case, a fashion star. Every year, I always put this ornament on the tree first. After that, I helped place the rest of the ornaments on the tree until there was no room for any more while joyfully singing Christmas carols with my family.

On Christmas morning, I woke up to a ton of presents under

the tree. Some for me, Brian, Ashley, Mom, and Dad. As I got up off the floor and turned around facing the kitchen, I noticed my dad holding a puppy with a pink bow on its head.

"You are already into your presents already," he said with a laugh. "How about receiving this present first?"

He gently handed me the adorable puppy and placed her in my arms. I could not believe I got a puppy for Christmas. I have wanted one for a very long time.

"You can name her anything you want," my dad said. "I hope you pick out a good one to fit her personality. She is such a frisky little thing."

I walked around the room while holding my Australian Shepherd puppy. Her coat was a mix of black, white, and gray. She had the most beautiful blue eyes that sparkled like the sun as it hits the pool water in the summer. So, I decided to name her Sparkle after her sparkling eyes. As I was still holding Sparkle, I took her outside to play. I placed her on the snow, and she started running around. I couldn't help but realize that Sparkle was so funny. She had a sense of humor and enjoyed being outside in the snow. This was her very first experience playing in the snow, and she enjoyed it. She was rolling around, jumping into the thick snow, and eating the snow that was falling from the sky. I guess Sparkle thought that the snow was food. Sparkle snapped at the snow as it fell close to her mouth. The image of her snapping the falling snow was so hilarious. I guess she didn't understand what was happening. Then she saw birds flying in the air, and she started barking at them. I watched her play for about an hour. When Sparkle was done playing, she ran to me, and I held her in my arms. I looked up into the sky and thought, *this is the best Christmas ever.*

CHAPTER EIGHT

Since it was a new year, I decided to dress a little differently. I mean, I am still going to wear pink, but I wanted to add a little flair to my outfit. My mom bought me a makeup kit for Christmas, so I thought this would be the best time to try it out. I walked over to my vanity table, sat down on my stool, and opened my smooth black box of makeup. The makeup box is a fancy and expensive kit; the only place you can order one like it is on the internet. The makeup box top opens like a jewelry box, and underneath the top, there are three drawers that are filled with eye shadow, blush, mascara, and eyeliner. The top is filled with brushes of many different sizes. I applied some mascara to my eyelashes, pink shadow to my eyelids, and blush to the apples of my cheeks so my makeup would complement the pink skirt that I had lying on my bed.

I put on my skirt and a white top, and all of a sudden, I heard this loud scream. I grabbed my shoes, put them on quickly, and ran downstairs.

Then I heard my mom say, "Don't run down the stairs, honey. You will fall and hurt yourself."

"I know, Mom," I said. "I rushed downstairs as fast as I could after I heard a scream coming from the outside. That person might be in serious trouble, and they may need my help."

I ran outside so fast that my mom could not get in another word. I stopped running and looked across the street. I couldn't believe what was happening right before my very eyes. Our sweet, older neighbor, Mrs. Birkly, was being robbed by a man in a black suit and mask.

"Give me all of your money," yelled the robber.

Mrs. Birkly's arm was shaking, and her voice was quivering. "But, I—I don't have any money, sir."

"Well, give me that bracelet," the robber shouted again as he pointed to her wrist.

"But . . . my husband gave this to me when we first met," cried Mrs. Birkly.

"I don't care; just give it to me," the robber exclaimed.

I had enough of this situation, so without thinking, I called out, "Hey you, leave her alone!"

The robber stopped what he was doing, glanced at me, then he started to run away.

Oh no, he is getting away. Somebody must stop him. He should not get away with robbing an older woman as sweet as Mrs. Birkly. No one should have to experience something like this; it is just awful. All of a sudden, I got this urge to chase after him. I ran so fast in my pink heels that I caught up to the robber, ran right into him, and knocked him to the ground. The robber hit the blacktop street so hard that it knocked out his breath. There we were, laying there with our faces looking downward at the street. I couldn't believe I landed on this guy's back as I fell. I didn't even want to be near this guy, but I had no choice in the matter. I wanted to keep him still so that he wouldn't hurt anyone else.

The robber turned his face to the side. "Can you . . . umm . . . get off . . . ah, my back?"

"No . . . you have to . . . um . . . stay here . . . uh . . . until the police arrive."

The robber and I were both out of breath and exhausted. We both could barely talk. He was still lying there as stiff as a board; he hardly moved a muscle. I sat up and used the robbers back as a seat to keep him on the ground. As this was all occurring, I thought about a few questions that I was worried about. What if he gets up? Or regains his energy? Will I be able to hold him here long enough before the cops arrive?

In just a few short minutes, a couple of police cars pulled up on both sides of the robber and me.

The policeman came out and said, "Young lady, you should be proud of yourself. You captured this criminal when we couldn't. How would you like to talk about your experience on the news? You are a hero and lucky to be alive."

"Well, I don't know . . . I am not really a hero," I told them. "I was just helping a friend in need."

"What is your name, young lady?" The officer pulled his cap downward.

"My name is Cynthia Adams."

"You have such a pretty name, Cynthia," said the officer. "You really shouldn't be modest; you saved the lives of everyone in this neighborhood."

"Thanks . . . I was just in the right place at the right time," I said. "I was just doing what I thought was the right thing to do."

I glanced up and saw my mom running toward me.

As she got closer to me, she yelled, "Are you okay, honey? I can't believe you actually captured this criminal. I am so glad I called the police in time. I was so afraid that you were going to get hurt by that horrible monster. I can see that you are okay now, thank goodness. I am so proud of you, sweetheart."

I thought it was funny that my mom called the robber a monster. Well, he is a monster for frightening an old lady like that. I hope he is put away in jail for life and never released.

"Thanks, Mom."

As I was looking at the situation at hand, I could not believe I captured him either. Where did I get all of this energy from? How did I get so brave? I wish I had an answer to both of these questions, but I had none.

The officer grabbed my hand and hoisted me up. I stood up, and suddenly I felt so tired, dizzy, and out of energy. I walked over to my mom and stood next to her while we watched the officer do his job. The officer started to search the robber while he was lying flat on his stomach to see if he had any weapons on him. First, the cop rummaged through the robber's pockets. No weapons there. Second, he patted the robber down and found no weapons there either. The police officer even took off the guy's shoes to check for weapons. He found no weapons in the robber's shoes. When the final search was completed, the cop lifted the robber onto his feet and handcuffed him. While having a hard grip on the robber's arms, the police officer walked him back to the car and placed him in the back seat. The officer took his clipboard out of the car, and as the officer turned around toward me, he seemed so familiar. He looks like someone I know, but I can't put a finger on it.

As I tried to figure out who the police officer looked like, I turned around to look at Mrs. Birkly. She looked so scared, and her arms were trembling. I walked over to her to give her some comfort. I felt so sorry for her because she lost her husband two years ago and now she lives alone with her four cats.

"Hi, Mrs. Birkly. Are you doing okay?"

"I am doing better, sweet child," said Mrs. Birkly. "Thanks for asking. Well . . . I am still shocked by what just happened to me. I am so glad that you heard me scream. I don't know if anyone else heard me or not, but I am so relieved that you came, sweetie. I wouldn't know what would have happened to me if you were not here. I might have . . . well . . . been a goner. I wouldn't have been able to fight him since my strength is not what it used to be."

We both leaned in and gave each other a hug.

"I am so glad that I could help," I said. "You are the sweetest lady in this neighborhood. I would do anything that I could to help you out. That's what friends are for, to help one another."

"Thank you, sweetie," Mrs. Birkly said as she smiled at me.

I started to walk away; then I thought of a question to ask Mrs. Birkly, so I turned back around. "Did the robber steal anything from you?"

"Only a bracelet, but that was just a material item. At least I am still alive, and I give all my thanks to you."

We hugged once more, then she turned around and walked back inside her house.

Instantly, I realized that I was going to be late for my first day back to school. So, I quickly ran down the street, passing three of my neighbors' homes, and I stopped in front of my house.

"I can't believe I am late for my first day back," I said out loud.

I opened the door, and I walked up the stairs to my room while thinking of what my classmates are saying about me at this minute. They probably think that I am so scared of Brittany that I chickened out from coming to school today. But that's not the case; I am not afraid of her. I just wish she would leave me alone. I know I shouldn't care about what my classmates think of me, but it really does bother me sometimes.

I turned right as I reached the top of the stairway and walked into my room. It wasn't as late as I thought. The time on the clock was 7:45. I couldn't believe how early it was, and I still had fifteen minutes to get to class. It just seemed like I was at the crime scene longer than that. I did all of that worrying for nothing.

Since I had about fifteen minutes till school started, I decided to check my appearance. I looked in the mirror that was in the left corner of my room to see if my outfit was presentable. To my surprise, I noticed that my knee was scraped up. I must have cut it when I knocked the robber to the ground. So, I went across the hall to the bathroom and dabbed some water on my cut. I put some medicine on and covered it with a bandage.

I walked back to my room and stood in front of my mirror again. I looked at my long, pink jacket that I got for Christmas. Something felt weird . . . almost like a rock was leaning on me. What is this odd feeling? My jacket pocket was bulging. What in the world? I reached in my pocket. There was the bracelet. The one that Mrs. Birkly loved and adored that was a gift from her deceased husband. How in the world did it get in my pocket? The robber must have wedged it in there . . . but how? No wonder the police officer didn't find anything. What am I going to do? I have to give this back to her, but I am running out of time. I am going to be really late. I brushed my hair quickly, and I quietly walked down the stairs as I put the bracelet in my jacket pocket.

As I reached the middle of the stairway, I noticed my mom standing in the living room waiting for me.

"That was such a brave thing you did, sweetie," said my mom.

My mom had this look on her face that really bothered me. That same expression that she always gives me when she wants me to do something that is not necessarily what I want to do. I always do what she suggests, but sometimes, I have to push myself to get them done. One time, she suggested to me that I had to clean the bathroom. I wasn't in trouble or anything; it's just one of the chores she asks me to do sometimes. I don't like cleaning the bathroom, but I did it. Sometimes I can figure out what she wants me to do ahead of time when I hear her talking to my dad when I chill on the stairs at night. But standing here now, I was uncertain of the favor she was about to ask.

"Mom, do you have something you want to say to me? I don't have a lot of time to talk. I don't want to be late for my first day back."

She looked at me with a serious expression on her face. "I am pretty sure you are not going to like what I have to say. So, please do not get upset with me. You know, when you captured the criminal this morning?"

"Yes. I do, Mom," I replied as I was figuring out how to get out of being framed by the robber.

"I called my boss at Local 6 News to report the story this morning, and I found out that a neighbor of ours captured you on film. They will air it sometime today. The only thing is that they requested to do an interview with you."

"Oh no, Mom. You did not do that," I cried out. "You told them I wouldn't do it, right?"

"Well . . . I wanted to ask you first," said my mom. "I knew you were going to get upset with me."

"I don't believe it," I hollered. "I do a good deed, and it goes all over the local news. Why, Mom? Why? I don't want to get media attention from your job. I just want to be a normal teenager. The kids at school already think I am weird."

"Sorry, honey," said my mom. "I just thought it would be a good story. I thought you would be honored to be on the news. I guess I was wrong about that. Honey, I don't think the students at school think you are weird."

"They do, Mom," I said as I thought about how hard it is to fit in at school. You are either one of the cool people, or you're not. Or maybe you're in the middle like me? But actually, it doesn't matter what group you fit into; the only thing that matters is that you are yourself with the people that are closest to you. I always think about this whenever I am having trouble fitting in with other people my age, and sometimes it is hard to take this advice to heart. I guess today is one of those days I am having trouble with my own advice. "They think I am weird just because I am not like the rest of the students. They don't like me because I am different. But I don't want to be like the rest of the students. It's okay, Mom. I accept your apology. I've got to leave for school . . . don't want to be late."

"See you later," my mom said as I closed the door and walked outside.

As soon as I got outside, my tears started dripping like a leaky faucet. I can't believe my mom did this to me. I wiped my eyes with a tissue that I got out of my purse and walked to the side yard. I grabbed my bike that was lying on the ground, walked over to the side gate, and said goodbye to Sparkles. I got on my bike, looked at my watch, and it said I still had five minutes to get to school. I pedaled faster, and the fresh, cool breeze felt so good on my face. The breeze dried my tears that I cried a few moments ago. The wind just had a calming effect on me, and I felt like all of my worries went away.

At school, everyone was hanging out outside by the fountain. Someone must have put soap in the fountain because I noticed bubbles rising up in the water. I saw the cheerleaders practicing on one side and the football players on the other. I walked up to the front of the building and locked up my bicycle. I started watching the football players practicing; they seemed really hyper. I saw Jason get a touchdown. We glanced at each other for a little while, but he neither waved nor smiled at me. I guess he is back to his popular self again.

I noticed that my friends Melanie, Melody, and Stanley were all sitting at a picnic table near the water fountain. Melody was sitting on top of the table, and Melanie and Stanley were sitting on the bench across from each other. I walked over to them, and as I passed the cheerleaders, I noticed that Brittany was staring at me with a furious expression on her face. When she saw me look her way, she curled up her nose and continued cheering.

"Hey, guys," I said as I sat down at the table with them. "What's wrong with Brittany? She has been staring at me since I got to school." I looked back at Brittany and then told my friends, "What's her problem?"

"She is angry at you because she got suspended," said Melanie.

Melody took another bite of her sausage biscuit and said, "She is probably jealous of your awesome outfit or maybe the real reason . . . Jason spending time with you."

"No, that's not the reason," said Stanley. "Brittany just has snot coming out of her nose."

Melanie, Melody, and I all said "gross" at the same time.

"Why are you so gross, Stanley?" Melanie asked as we all started to laugh.

"I am not gross; it is just what I saw," Stanley said as he picked up a tater tot to eat and shrugged his shoulders. "I just tell it like it is."

Melody and I couldn't stop laughing.

The cheerleaders walked by us with Brittany in the lead as usual.

"Oh, what are you guys laughing at?" Brittany asked as she twirled her hair. "Tell me—or else. It so better not be about me."

"Oh, Brittany," said Stanley. "Why does it always have to be about you? You are not a princess like you think you are. It does not matter if we said something about you or not. Even if we did say something about you, it would not ruin your reputation of being a popular brat."

I could not believe my shy friend Stanley is actually standing up to my enemy. Way to go, Stanley!

"Wow, Stanley," said Brittany. "I have to give you props for standing up to me. I never thought that you, especially, felt this way about me. I could expect that from Cindy and Mallory, but not from you. I thought we were good friends, Stanley."

"Uh . . . " said Stanley. "I wouldn't consider us . . . "

Melody was ticked off at Brittany and interrupted Stanley. "Um . . . my name is Melody."

"Oh, whatever," said Brittany as she rolled her eyes at Melody. Brittany twirled her hair again and looked at Stanley. "Hey, Stanley. Would you like to sit at the popular table with us during lunch?"

I can't believe that turned her on. Oh, wait! I know what she is doing. She is trying to make my life more miserable by hitting on my friend Stanley.

"Sorry, I am going to have to turn you down on that offer," said Stanley. "I am going to eat lunch with my best friends."

"Well . . . I am sorry to hear that, Stanley. You would have enjoyed spending time with us. Suit yourself," said Brittany as she and her posse walked toward the building.

Brittany paused near the entrance of the school and looked over her shoulder. "Stanley, you are one of us now." After that, she winked at Stanley, and then she continued walking toward her group.

Melody, Melanie, Stanley, and I all were in shock and confused about what just happened. Or, what did just happen was more the question.

We all shrugged our shoulders as Brittany caught up to her cheerleader friends.

"We all are so proud of you, Stanley," I said as I looked at him and smiled. I looked at Brittany a few times. I was worried that she would come back over here. I didn't want her to bother my friends again.

"Yeah, it is about time that one of us stood up to that girl," said Melody as she turned around to look at Brittany talking to her squad.

"I am confused," said Melanie. "Was Brittany trying to hit on Stanley? Or was I just day-dreaming while that was happening?"

"Yes, she was hitting on me," said Stanley in an exasperating manner. "I would not go out with her if she was the last girl on earth. Besides, why would I go out with her when I got these three beautiful girls right here?"

"Aw, Stanley . . . you are so sweet," said Melanie and I together.

"Okay, Stanley," Melody said as she rolled her eyes. "Don't push it. I am not much for the sweet, sappy stuff, especially when it comes to my life."

We all laughed so hard that tears came to our eyes.

Melody, Melanie, and I all stood up beside Stanley and gave him a big hug; then, all of a sudden, I was beginning to get worried. Stanley thinks all of us are beautiful, but why doesn't my crush think I am?

Stanley looked at me and asked, "Are you okay? Is something wrong?"

I looked back up at the football players practicing. "I wish Jason would think I was beautiful." I sighed.

"I am sure he does, somewhere inside of him, but he's probably not good with expressing his feelings," said Stanley. "Sometimes, if you have a crush on somebody, it will work out, but other times, it doesn't. That's the way life is sometimes. If you are supposed to be with someone, that one you are meant to be with . . . it will just happen."

Stanley patted my hand with his, and then he looked up at me and smiled. I didn't know Stanley was such a romantic. I always enjoy learning new things about my friends.

Just as soon as I saw Brittany walk through the door, the bell rang for class. I was hoping that the bell would have rung earlier before Brittany came over to flirt with Stanley, but that didn't happen. Oh, anyway, I was so proud of Stanley for standing up to Brittany. She so deserved it; if it weren't for Stanley being with us, she would pick on us even more than she does now.

I did not think this day could get any worse, but it certainly did as soon as I walked in the front door. The cafeteria is the room you enter when you first walk in, and they have televisions hanging from the ceiling playing the local news. And guess what they were reporting? You guessed it—the robbery that happened this morning. I just stood there in front of the television, in shock. I never thought I would rescue someone or be on television. I know I did a good deed, but I did not want to be recognized for it. I was just in the right place at the right time, and I was glad I was there to help my neighbor out.

Melanie and Melody were also standing beside me as I was gazing in shock at the television.

"In our small town, a local teenage girl saved an elderly woman from being robbed," said the blonde reporter. "The elderly woman, Mrs. Birkly, was frightened for her life and unsure if anyone was going to help her. Then in the blink of an eye, a young girl named Cynthia chased the robber and knocked him straight to the ground. What a sight that was . . . what a brave little girl. Now, let's talk to the woman who endured this tragedy. Mrs. Birkly, how do you feel?"

"I am frightened, actually; my limbs are still trembling," Mrs. Birkly replied. "I don't know what I would have done without Cynthia. She saved my life, and I thank her so much."

"They did capture the robber, and he is in police custody," the blonde reporter stated. "Did any valuables you own get stolen?"

"Only a bracelet that my husband gave me when we first dated," Mrs. Birkly spoke. "But the robber can have it; as long as I am alive, that's all that counts."

"Unfortunately, we couldn't speak to the young girl who saved Mrs. Birkly," the blonde reporter stated as a man came up to her and whispered something in her ear. "We just found out the bracelet is still missing . . . we hope we can give you an update on this as soon as possible. Now, let's replay the video of Cynthia saving the day. This is Barbara Marks reporting for Local 6 News."

"Boy, Cynthia!" said Melanie. "I can't believe you knocked that guy down."

"Where did you get all of that extra strength and energy?" asked Melody.

My friends were just as shocked as I was about this incident. This is the scariest and bravest thing I have ever done in my life. I don't know how I became so brave all of a sudden. Or how I got enough energy to knock this guy down, but I did it. I just stood there, continuing to watch the screen while I thought over all of this.

"I can't believe I did this either, guys," I said as I continued to ponder. "I don't know where I got the extra energy from . . . it just came to me."

I was hoping the answer that I gave them was sufficient. That was the only answer I could come up with since I was unsure of the answer myself. But as soon as Melanie and Melody both wrapped one of their arms around the back of my neck, I knew they accepted my answer. I have such great friends; they are always there for me no matter what is happening in my life. I stopped looking at the screen when I just couldn't handle watching it anymore. And I noticed that my friends quit watching as well. I guess they were just as overwhelmed as I was at that moment. I turned around the same time Melody and Melanie did, and we were surprised to see a group of students staring at us. Well, they weren't staring at my friends; they were staring at me. I started to feel very uncomfortable and nervous.

"Can you guys walk me to my first class? I would really appreciate it." I let my eyes wander around the room again. "Why is everyone looking at me like I am some kind of weirdo?"

Melody and Melanie said together, "Sure, we will."

"It seems the students here have never seen a celebrity before," said Melody as she stared at the other students as we walked by them. "It's rare to see a famous person in this small town."

"I am not a celebrity or a really famous person, but okay," I said as we all started to laugh. Melody always knows what to say to cheer me up.

We walked together down the hall to my first class, which was science.

As we got closer to my class, there was a small group of five students standing around chatting in the hall. They continued to chat until they noticed that I looked familiar. They must have seen the news as well. Just as I walked by, they stopped talking and started to stare at me with the craziest, dazed expressions on their faces.

As soon as Melody saw them looking, she said, "What are you guys staring at? You guys have nothing better to do than to stare at my friend. Or have you never seen a brave person before? My friend has had a rough morning; just leave her alone. You have no idea what she has been through today."

After Melody responded to them, they quickly and automatically stopped staring and continued on with their conversation.

"I can't believe all of this is happening to me in one day," I said as I frowned at Melody and Melanie. "Everyone in this school seems to be making my heroic deed more dramatic than it actually was; just what we need . . . more drama in this school. I don't know what I would have done without you guys. I probably would have cried and gone home. Thank you both for being there for me."

"You're welcome, Cynthia," Melody replied. "That's what friends are for."

"Yes," said Melanie. "We are here for you anytime you need us. Don't ever forget that."

"I won't forget," I said when I finally arrived at the door of my science class. Melody and Melanie stood by the door as I walked into the classroom, so I turned around to face them.

"I will see you both at lunch at our same table, right?"

Melanie nodded, and Melody gave me a thumbs up in agreement. We all smiled and gave each other a hug. We all pulled back, and I waved goodbye to them as they went on their way to class.

I peeked out into the hallway, and I noticed that Jason and Brittany were coming in the direction of my classroom. I sure hope she is not one of my classmates this semester. That would drive me crazy. I already see enough of her in the mornings, in the halls, and at lunch. I bet she is in my class. As weird as this day has been for me, I had a feeling it was going to get worse. The closer she got to me, the more my hunch increased. I wished I was wrong, but she is definitely in my class. Jason and Brittany tried to get past me and almost knocked me down, trying to get into the room. I almost fell on the floor, but instead of falling, I held my balance and dropped my science book on the floor instead. The science book hit the floor so hard that it almost sounded like a person jumping off a diving board. Jason heard the thump of the book hitting the floor and slowly tried to pick it up at the same time as I did.

As he was still bent over halfway holding the book, he said, "Here you go. I am so sorry that we knocked your book out of your hands." He looked at me with his perfect blue eyes and smiled when he recognized who I was.

"Jason! What are you doing?" interrupted Brittany without acknowledging that I was standing by Jason.

"I am just helping this girl pick up her book," said Jason.

"Well, hurry up," Brittany said. "I want to give my love a kiss goodbye."

I grabbed my book from Jason's hand and quietly said, "Thank you."

Jason smiled again and nodded at me, which was his way of saying you're welcome silently without Brittany hearing. He walked over to Brittany and kissed her on the lips. The kiss was so romantic—almost like the end of a fairytale story when the prince finally finds his girl. But to me, this ending was quite different in the way I saw it. In my view, it seemed like this prince has found the wrong girl in the end. I am not saying that I should be that girl, but I think Jason deserves someone better than Brittany. After the kiss, he waved goodbye and went on his way to his next class.

I took my seat in the second row, second seat from the back, on the left side of the classroom. Brittany took a seat in the third row, which was the second seat toward the front of the classroom. The rest of the students filled up the unoccupied seats.

"Hello, class. My name is Professor Whittlebottom."

I hear all of my classmates start to snicker around me.

The professor clears his throat. "Ummm," He looked up at the class. When the students stopped snickering and became quiet and attentive, Mr. Whittlebottom continued on with his conversation.

"I teach science here and at the University of Bluesville. I have a master's degree in science and a minor in psychology. I have been happily married for fifteen years and have two sons. But, I don't want to bore you with my life story, so let's get started learning, shall we? Today, we are going to cover gravity. Does anyone know what gravity is?"

"Gravity is what keeps us from floating in the air," said a girl in the back of the classroom.

"Yes, that is correct," said the professor. "You are on the right track. Gravity, or gravitation, is the pull on bodies toward the earth's center. Gravity is what keeps our feet on the ground."

"Cynthia should know a lot about gravity, the way she knocked the robber down this morning."

Oh, brother, I can't believe this. I thought this event was over. She just doesn't know when to stop, does she?

"That was really inappropriate to interrupt me while I was giving an important lecture." He glanced down at his list to look at the names. "I don't know everyone's names yet, but you must be Brittany. I have heard a lot about you. If you interrupt my class one more time, I will send you directly to the principal's office. Is that clear, Brittany?"

Brittany's face turned bright red, and she said, "Yes, sir."

After the teacher supposedly thought Brittany learned her lesson, he continued speaking. "Is there gravity on the moon? The astronauts on the moon experience less gravity. How is that?" Mr. Whittlebottom drew a small representation of the moon on the chalkboard, and then he picked up his pointer to explain the image. "Well, the moon is so small and has less mass, so it pulls with less gravity." He circled his pointer around the moon drawing. "So, standing on the moon, you would experience seventeen percent of the gravity that you would experience here on the earth." Then he wrote "17 percent" right next to his moon drawing.

As I was half-listening to the teacher, I could not believe that Brittany was actually embarrassed by something she had done. I could not wait till class was over to tell Melody, Melanie, and Stanley the great news.

As the class was coming to a close, I glanced at the clock, and it was only ten minutes till lunchtime. I could not wait till lunch to eat; I was starving. And plus, I had some juicy gossip to tell. I looked over at Brittany in the third row; she was filing her nails and polishing them at the same time. I could not believe her; she acted as if nothing happened. If I got yelled at by a teacher, I would be almost in tears, but I am not Brittany. Then I noticed that she stopped polishing her nails for a moment, grabbed her cell phone out of the side pocket of her purse, and began typing a message.

Cynthia could not view the message, but it read:

> Hey, sweetie. Can you meet me at my classroom in about two minutes, so that we can walk to lunch together? I want the whole student body class to see us as a couple, so we can get nominated for the King and Queen of the Beyond the Sea Dance. You wouldn't want the queen to make an entrance by herself, would you? Love you, handsome.
> Your girl, Brittany.

I saw her click the send button, and she continued painting her nails while waiting for a reply. I couldn't imagine what was so important that Brittany couldn't wait to say it in person.

While Cynthia was waiting for the bell to ring for lunch, Jason was in woodshop class. Jason was building a chair for an assignment when he received a text message from someone. Jason shut off his equipment and took off his goggles. He placed his hand into his right pocket and grabbed his cell phone. He glanced at the screen and noticed it was from Brittany. He rolled his eyes while he read the message.

> Hey, sweetie. Can you meet me at my classroom in about two minutes, so that we can walk to lunch together? I want the whole student body class to see us as a couple, so we can get nominated for the King and Queen of the Beyond the Sea Dance.

He skipped the next few lines; then, he noticed it was signed, "love, Brittany."

He closed his phone and threw it across the room. "Why do girls always care about being queens of dances? She has won every year. I am so tired of being this fake person. I want to be the real me."

His friend, Ryan, who is also in woodshop class, tried to cheer up Jason the best he knew how. "I don't know, dude. I don't understand what you are so upset about. You have the life that every guy in Bluesville High wants. You are popular, dating a beautiful girl. What else do you want?"

"Man, I guess you are right," said Jason. "I just wish I could be the real me with her."

Jason walked across the room to pick up his phone, which luckily wasn't broken. He opened his inbox and began to type his message.

> Sure, honey. I will be right there. I wouldn't want you to make an entrance by yourself.

He signed his name and clicked send. "Well, guys, I have to go. I don't want to keep the princess waiting."

All of a sudden, a spread of laughter poured through the room, starting with Ryan, and then the rest of the guys followed.

After the laughter became less rowdy, Ryan yelled, "Go get your princess."

Suddenly Jason remembered something while he was standing in the doorway, and he turned around. He placed his index finger up and looked directly at his friend. "Oh! Ryan, do we have football practice this week?"

"Yeah, man," said Ryan. "We have practice every day this week. Our coach is being extra tough with our workout and practice this week. But, if we win our game on Friday, the coach will buy us pizza. The pizza is definitely worth that."

"Then we must win," said Jason.

"There is the guy we like," said Ryan and all of the other guys.

Meanwhile, back at Mr. Whittlebottom's classroom, Brittany received a text message back from Jason, and she was thrilled.

I didn't realize who she was talking to until Jason showed up at the door. I should have known; those two are always together. Those two stick together like peanut butter and jelly. Then I started to giggle. I just started to stare at his face, thinking, *wow, he is so handsome*. It was like the sun enveloped around him like he was an angel. I could almost hear a choir singing in the background until it stopped and disappeared when the bell rang right at the best part of my wonderful daydream. I wish my daydream could have lasted longer, but I was in a rush to see my friends. I grabbed my books and headed to lunch to talk to my friends about "the incident" that happened in science class today.

I ran as fast as a cheetah to the cafeteria, and when I got in line, Brittany was ahead of me. I was like, of all the students in this school, she had to be the one in front of me. I was trying to be very quiet, so she would not know that I was there. I was already having a weird sort of day. I did not want to make the day even worse, so I just listened to her conversation.

"Oh my goodness," said Brittany in her best valley girl voice. "I am like having the best day ever. Well, except for this morning, but anyway, you will never guess what happened to me."

"Ooooh! Did you get like . . . a thousand-dollar shopping spree for clothes?" said Brittany's best friend, Mandy. "That would be like, so totally awesome."

"That would be awesome, but no. Any more guesses?" asked Brittany as she waited patiently for Crystal to answer.

"Did you get your nails done?" Crystal asked.

"No, I get my nails done every week. I just finished polishing my nails in science class. Aren't they beautiful?" Brittany showed her friends her bright, shiny, purple fingernails. "Okay, I will tell you. Guess who is going to the Beyond the Sea Dance with Jason?"

With their eyes and mouths wide open, Mandy and Crystal turned to each other to see if the other one knew the answer to Brittany's question. With no clue of the answer, they both looked back at Brittany with blank stares on their faces.

"Okay, I will say it," said Brittany. "Me!"

"I am so glad he asked you out," said Mandy. "He was taking like, forever."

"He just needed a little push in the right direction," said Brittany confidently.

"Now, we will have to go shopping for a fabulous dress," said Crystal. "I know the perfect place to take you."

"You just read my mind, Crystal," said Brittany.

I could not believe what I was hearing. How could this be? I thought he was going to ask me, not her. I went from being super excited to super depressed in exactly three minutes. I slowly grabbed my pizza with fries and went to pay for it. I finally got out of line and just stood by the wall.

Melody, Melanie, and Stanley were all sitting at our usual lunch table. Melanie was drawing in her sketchbook. Melody was eating her fries and watching her sister draw. And Stanley was eating a slice of pizza and reading a sports magazine.

"Where is Cynthia?" asked Melanie as she placed her pencil down on the table and looked up at Melody and Stanley. "I am worried about her. She is usually here by now."

Stanley placed down his pizza and glared across the room. "Look, I see her." Stanley pointed in front of him. "She is over there by that wall."

Melanie twisted her head around to see Cynthia. "Why is she just sitting there by herself?" Melanie turned back around to look at her friends. "What happened to her?"

"I don't know," said Stanley. "She looks pretty bummed."

"Cynthia told me in a text message that she had some exciting news to tell us," said Melody. "But I think something else happened since she last texted me. She looks so depressed."

"She acts like she doesn't even want to sit with us," said Melanie.

"Yeah, I can see that." All of a sudden, Stanley became very worried. "Has she been snatched by the popular crowd? Did they turn her against us?"

"No, weirdo," said Melody. "I just think someone upset her, that's all. You should know Cynthia better than that; she would never sit with anyone else besides us."

"I am not a weirdo," said Stanley.

"Well, actually . . . you are a weirdo," said Melanie. "But that's why we like you."

Melody stood up from her seat and noticed Cynthia sliding her back down the wall to sit on the floor.

"I am going to check on her," said Melody. "I will be right back."

Melody walked from her table to where Cynthia was and sat down right beside her.

"Are you okay?" Melody asked in a concerned voice. "You seemed so excited when you sent me a text earlier. What happened?"

"I am down in the dumps, but I will be all right. A lot has happened to me since I last texted you."

"Would it help if we talked about it?" Melody asked.

"Yes, actually; that would be great."

I walked over with Melody and sat down at our table. All of my friends were looking at me with the saddest expressions on their faces. I just felt so depressed, and their faces weren't helping much. I wanted to talk to them, but I just wasn't in the right mood. None of them said anything for about two minutes; then I noticed Melanie tilting her head sideways to look at me. Maybe she would break the silence.

"What happened?" Melanie asked.

"Our ears are ready to listen," said silly Stanley.

I giggled when he said that. Now that the silence was broken by Stanley and Melanie, I was starting to feel more like myself. I started to perk up, and I started to tell them everything.

"Well, this morning, while the teacher was lecturing about gravity, Brittany made a rude remark about me knocking down the robber this morning."

"She shouldn't have done that," said Melanie.

"Then Professor Whittlebottom told her that he knew who she was and fussed at her for making that remark," I said. "Then he stated if she ever made an outburst like that again, he would send her directly to the principal's office. Boy was her face red."

"I would have liked to have seen her get embarrassed," said Melody. "I thought she never got embarrassed by anything."

"Yeah . . . I got to witness it all," I replied as I snickered.

"Was her face as red as my library book?" Melanie asked.

"No, actually, her face was red as a rose."

"I wish I could have seen Professor Whittlebottom fuss at her," said Stanley. "I would be laughing in the back of the classroom so loud that I would probably be sent to the principal's office."

"Yes . . . and I will be right in the principal's office with you," said Melody, laughing. "The teacher would send me right behind you because I won't be able to stop laughing either. That's some funny stuff."

"Yeah, actually, that would be funny; funnier than any show on television," I said. "Now, it's time for the bad news, well, for me, it is. I just heard from Brittany while standing in line that she and Jason are going to the dance together."

"Ugh . . . ladies always talk about their crushes when I am around," said Stanley. "I am going outside to chill in the fresh air for a bit. I need a break from all of this girl stuff."

"Okay," all the girls said together.

"You know you love all this girl stuff," shouted Melody.

"Yeah . . . I do," said Stanley.

Melody, Melanie, and I chuckled about Stanley's love for girl talk.

As Stanley was leaving, Melanie became serious. "I am so sorry, Cynthia. I can't imagine how you feel. I haven't had a secret crush on a guy as long as you have. Maybe he will change his mind, dump Brittany, and take you."

"I thought Jason said he wanted to take you to the dance," said Melody.

"Yes, Jason did say that he would like to take me, but I guess he or someone else changed his mind."

"I bet it was Ryan; he always likes convincing someone to do it his way," said Melody.

"I don't know who convinced him, but that doesn't matter to me anymore," I said. "He is going with Brittany and no one else. It has been this way for years. He is never going to be the person that I know and love. Jason is always going to hang out with the popular crowd. He will never admit to anyone that he likes me. I guess I just realized the truth—that Jason and I will never be together."

I just laid my head down on the table and started to cry. Why did it take me so long to figure this out? I guess I just enjoyed daydreaming of what might have been if Jason was himself.

CHAPTER NINE

The Spring Fling: Beyond the Sea Dance was just around the corner. I had so many things to do in so little time. The dance was just weeks away. I wanted to get a new dress, new shoes, and a matching purse. I was hoping I could find something pink since pink is my favorite color, but if not, I could find something blue to match the theme of the dance. Since today is Friday, my mom told me that she would take me shopping as soon as she came home from work.

As soon as I got to school, all of the excitement I had about the dance just suddenly disappeared. I just realized I was dateless, and Brittany was still going to the dance with Jason. It was like the horrible nightmare just reappeared all over again. I was waiting for the first class bell to ring when all of a sudden, I saw Jason and Brittany kissing in the corner of the lunchroom.

I walked over to our usual table to sit down next to my friends Melody, Melanie, and Stanley.

I must have looked upset when I sat down at our table when Melody asked, "Did you see the two love birds smooching?"

"Of course, I did," I told her in disgust.

"There should be a law restricting that kind of kissing between two people that don't belong together," said Melody.

We all started laughing at the same time.

"Melody, you come up with the craziest stuff, but that's what I like about you," said Stanley.

"I wish I could make a law, but there's nothing I can do about it," I said. "Jason loves Brittany, and Brittany loves Jason. I just have to sit here, ignore the situation, and move on with my life."

"Cynthia, I don't think they love each other as much as you think they do," said Melody. "I have heard a little gossip around this school lately. They are only dating because both of them are popular, and they are a shoo-in to win as king and queen of the upcoming dance."

"I wouldn't doubt that what you heard was the truth," I said. "Knowing Brittany, she will probably do anything to be the queen of the dance."

"That should be you kissing him, not her," said Melanie as she turned her head around to look at Jason and Brittany making out. "I have a feeling that Jason will come around. You just have to be patient."

"How can you be so sure?" I sighed.

"I just know," said Melanie.

"I sure hope you are right," I said as I waited patiently for the bell to ring.

The bell rang, and all of the students headed to the gym. We are missing our first two classes due to a pep rally for our football team. I sure hope that I don't see Jason or Brittany there, but I know I will since they are both important athletes for our school. The football team can't win without Jason, and as a matter of fact, the cheerleaders would be lousy without Brittany. I can't believe I had that thought about Brittany, but it is true, unfortunately. To clear my mind off of Jason and Brittany, I just spoke the first thought that came to my mind.

"I am so glad it is Friday," I told my friends as we continued walking to the gym.

"Yeah," said Stanley. "Friday is the last day of the week before the weekend."

We all laughed because Stanley has a silly sense of humor, but we love him for it.

"The best part of this Friday is that we get to miss our first two classes to go to the pep rally."

"I know . . . we get to watch the cheerleaders cheer and see the football players practice," said Melody. "But hey, it's better than going to class."

"Yeah, I know what you mean," I replied. "I am so glad that I am missing science class for this; at least Brittany can't do anything to me here, right?"

"I think you are safe from Brittany," said Stanley. "She will be too busy cheering to pick on you in there."

As we all leisurely walked into the gym, the four of us proceeded to the bleachers on the right side of the room. We walked all the way to the top. These seats are much comfier than the others, and plus, they have extra padding to rest your back on. However, when we got there, there was only room for three of us at the top. So, Stanley sat in front of us, and we sat at the very top.

"I usually don't go to games because I'd rather be at home watching television, but right now, I am starting to crave a hot dog," said Stanley. "I don't know why I am so hungry. I ate a big breakfast this morning."

"I know, being at a game makes me hungry, too," said Melody. "I don't have much, but I do have a few pieces of gum and a chocolate bar."

"I will take half of the chocolate bar," said Stanley.

Melody broke off half of her chocolate bar and handed it to Stanley. He grabbed the chocolate bar and took a bite out of it. Melody looked at me and showed me her chocolate bar.

"Do you want the last piece of my chocolate bar, Cynthia?"

I shook my head from side to side while looking down at the floor. "No, thank you. Melody, you can go ahead and eat the rest."

"Okay," said Melody. "More for me to enjoy."

While still looking downward, I turned my head to the left and caught a glimpse of Melody shrugging her shoulders. Before I decided to look back down at the floor, I took a second glimpse of Melody. She was chewing a piece of her gum while holding her chocolate bar in her hand.

I slowly glanced up from looking at the floor, and I saw Jason looking around the room. *Was he looking for me?* I wondered. When he glanced in my direction, I waved and smiled at him.

"Why is he acting like he doesn't see me?" I asked.

"Well . . . Cynthia," said Melody, "he is popular now. He doesn't know you exist."

"He surely does know that I exist, but he is too afraid to admit it," I said. Afterward, I realized that both of us were right, and I just let out a disappointed "oh," and I placed my hands on my cheeks.

The vice-principal of our school, Mr. Long, stood in the middle of the gymnasium. "Today is our first time in a playoff game. It's our first time to meet and beat the mighty dogs," said Mr. Long. "Are we ready to beat them?"

The whole crowd of students screamed, "Yes!"

"All right, cheerleaders, show us what you've got," said the vice principal.

In a straight line, all of the cheerleaders came out before the pep band started to play. While still in line, they stood in the center of the gymnasium, and their eyes looked toward the floor. A bouncy, upbeat tune began to play, and all of the cheerleaders held their hands on their sides, and they looked straight ahead. Brittany raised her arms over her head and moved her head slightly to the right. The next cheerleader behind Brittany moved her head slightly to the left, and it continued in that manner till the last cheerleader was shown. They all scattered around the gymnasium floor while clapping their hands, and they began to pump up the crowd with their pop, freestyle dancing. Then, all of the football players, including Jason, began to dance with the cheerleaders. Melanie, Stanley, and I got up to dance, and we moved our feet from side to side. And Stanley even threw in a raise the roof, which made us girls laugh. However, the only one of us that wasn't dancing was Melody; she was too busy enjoying her candy bar. The football players began showing us their passes, making touchdowns, showing us their determination to win tonight's game. I was enjoying this so much. I wish this pep rally would last all day, but it didn't. The two hours of fun came to a close, and we all had to head back to our third class. I was lucky that I did not have to leave because my class was in the gym. I said goodbye to my friends, and I told them I would see them at lunch.

I sat down on the bench in the first row and relaxed for a few minutes. I was trying to calm down from all of this excitement I just experienced. At that moment, I decided I would go inside the girl's locker room to change into my light blue shirt and dark blue shorts. Our school made our gym uniforms this color because when you are in shallow water, the water appears to be lighter. The farther away you get from the shallow water, the water gets darker or appears darker.

As soon as I stepped into the locker room, I heard a girl talking.

"I can't believe her, Crystal. Waving at my man. She is never going to quit trying to steal him away from me."

It was Brittany's voice. How dare she say such things. I am not trying to steal him away. I stood there quietly behind the wall and continued to listen.

Another girl began to speak, and her voice was different than Brittany's, so it must have been Crystal. "Maybe she does just want to be friends with him. I don't see anything wrong with them being friends."

I was beginning to like Crystal; she seemed nice. I peeked around the corner, watching all three of the girls walk up to the sinks to brush their hair. The girls imitated one another as they looked in their mirrors and started to brush their silky, shiny hair.

"No!" Brittany shouted as she moved her brush away from her hair. "I think she wants to date him."

"Come on, Brittany; calm down," spoke Mandy as she pointed her brush at the mirror. "Look at you, then look at her. Do you think he is seriously going to dump you for her?"

What's that supposed to mean? Are they talking about me? I looked down at my clothes. Are they trying to say that I am not as pretty as Brittany to date a guy like Jason? Well, I have never considered myself beautiful, but what they are saying about me isn't fair. Jason may be attracted to me or any other girl in this school, for that matter. They really shouldn't place people in categories by their looks. It's just not right. I think everyone is attractive in their own way.

"Yeah, you are right, girls," said Brittany as she placed her brush on the sink. "I have nothing to worry about." Then all three of the girls walked through the side door and went out into the hallway.

I peeked around the corner to make sure Brittany and her friends weren't around. I looked around the lockers, and I saw no one. I quickly ran to my locker, number 112, and got out my clothes.

Then, all of a sudden, as I was grabbing my clothes, I heard a noise at the side door. "Oh, girls, I forgot my brush," said a girl's voice. "I am going back into the locker room to get it."

The door slowly opened and creaked. "Girls, can you get me something to drink? I am really thirsty," said the girl to her friends. I peeked around my locker, and I saw that the door was opened all the way. I saw the girl's shadow first, then I saw her. It was Brittany again.

I quickly threw all of my clothes back into my locker and lowered myself down, so she wouldn't catch a glimpse of me.

"Oh, there it is . . . on the sink where I left it," spoke Brittany.

While I sat in the squatting position, I quietly sent a text to my friends:

Hey guys, you will never guess what I heard in the
locker room. Will tell about it later at lunch.

What I forgot about my phone was that it beeps when it sends a message. And guess who, out of all people, heard it. Yeah, you guessed it . . . Brittany.

"Who is in here?" Brittany shouted. "There is supposed to be no one in here right now."

Come on, I thought, *like Brittany ever follows the rules.* Since no one is supposed to be in here, why was Brittany allowed to be in here earlier? Maybe she has special privileges in here since she is a cheerleader, but I am just guessing, though.

I stood quietly by my locker while Brittany was trying to find the person hiding in here. But what she didn't know was that it was me. Brittany looked around the locker room and found no one. I guess I hid pretty well. So, she decided to quit looking and walked out into the hallway. I quietly grabbed my clothes again and went into one of the stalls to change. I did not want anyone coming in while I was changing. I put on my gym uniform and headed to the gymnasium.

After school let out, my mom picked me up to go dress shopping. I was so excited to go since I love fashion and trying on clothes. I have been waiting for this moment all my life.

As we were driving down the road a bit, my mom and I noticed a big sign that read, "LeAnna's Fashion Boutique," so we decided to check it out. We parked our car and entered the fashion store. I stepped in before my mom did. I was so amazed at how beautiful the store was inside. The outside of the building wasn't much, but the inside was delicate, enchanting, and sparkly. I stood there admiring the décor. I felt like this was the place where almost anything could happen.

When you first walk in, you see this giant, shiny chandelier hanging from the ceiling. The walls were covered with different colored gemstones all throughout the store. The walls were painted in turquoise, which made the room even more enchanting. The flower hanging by the door was made of colored glass. The floor was white mixed in a pattern with some that were made of clear glass. Inside the clear tiles, you could see a single red rose. On the right side of the room, there was the checkout counter where the owner of the store was stationed.

A young brunette lady who was wearing a brown business suit came out from behind the counter and started to approach us.

"Hello, my name is LeAnna. Welcome to my boutique. Is there anything I may help you with this evening?"

"Well, actually, there is something you can help us with," said my mom. "My daughter Cynthia is going to her spring fling, and she needs something pretty to wear."

"Well, you have come to the right place, then," LeAnna said. "Do you prefer a certain color, or will any color suffice?"

"My favorite color is pink, but I am willing to try on anything."

"Very well. I will let you browse," spoke LeAnna in her soft-spoken voice. "And if you need anything, don't hesitate to ask me."

My mom and I started browsing for the perfect dress. Even though I didn't have a date, I still wanted to dress up. I tried on a purple dress, then a red one and neither of them fit right. As I was trying on my third dress, which was green, by the way, my mom started asking me questions.

"Honey, I wanted to ask you something," spoke my mom.

"Sure, Mom. You can ask me anything."

"I am not sure how to ask this, honey, because I don't want to make you feel uncomfortable," said my mother. "I know you have been crushing on this guy named Jason since you have started high school. Is he going to take you to the dance?"

After she asked her question, there were a couple of minutes of silence. I don't know how this conversation could get any more awkward. Well, Brittany could be in this very dressing room trying on dresses and overhearing our conversation, but that wasn't the case here. Now, I went back to thinking about how to answer her question. Even though I still thought this was a very awkward topic to discuss while trying on clothes.

In the midst of the silence, my mother spoke again. "Honey, are you still in there?"

While I was holding up the top of my green dress, I started to stare in the mirror, picturing myself looking like a princess. All I needed was a tiara and some nice heels, and I will resemble one of my favorite fairytale princesses from my childhood. But this dress was too big, by the way, but it still looked beautiful. I just had to find the one that fits just perfectly. I stopped staring in the mirror and realized that my mom was talking to me.

"No, Mom, he is going . . . "

Before I could continue to say more, LeAnna barged into the entrance of the dressing room area. "Are you finding anything you like?"

"No . . . not yet, but we are still looking," said my mother.

I was so glad that LeAnna interrupted when she did because I really did not want to talk about Jason. I was so excited about finding a dress that I did not want to get depressed about not having a date. Anyway, I was not actually going alone. Melody, Melanie, Stanley, and I are all going to the dance together. There is nothing wrong with going with friends if you don't have a date. I was surprised that Melody wanted to go to this dance; usually, dances and wearing dresses are not her things. She is such a tomboy that she would rather wear jeans and a t-shirt than wear a girly dress. I can't wait to see what she wears to the spring fling.

My mom had a confused tone in her voice. "I don't remember what we were talking about, but I guess it wasn't that important since I don't remember it. Does the dress you have on now fit you?"

"No, Mom . . . it doesn't fit."

I put that dress with the others that didn't fit right, and I started looking for another. I came upon this dress in the corner of the room. It was so perfect, pretty, and pink. I grabbed it and took it into the dressing room to try on. The top of the dress was sparkly pink, and the bottom half was white silk. I tried it on, and it fit perfectly. After trying on so many dresses, I found the perfect one.

"Mom, I finally found the dress that I want to buy and wear to the dance," I yelled excitedly.

My mom walked into my dressing room and looked at me from head to toe. "You look so beautiful in this dress. You look like a princess. This dress fits you so perfectly. You are a vision in white and pink."

Right then and there, I knew I found the perfect dress when she gave me those compliments. My mom went to pay for my dress, and all I was thinking as I was standing by the mirror was, *wait till Jason sees me now.*

CHAPTER TEN

The long-awaited day has finally arrived where all of the girls at Bluesville High can dress up as princesses, and all of the guys have to be charming and look like a prince. I can't wait to see the décor and how everything is going to be set up. This is the day I have been waiting for since I was a child when I first saw my sister getting ready for her dance. I remember standing there beside her as I watched her put her whole outfit together. I thought she looked amazing. I remember this one dress in particular she wore; it was this long, shiny, purple gown. She wore gold shoes and earrings to complement her dress. I guess my sister inspired my fashion taste because I like to dress up every day, but today is extra special; it is the high school dance.

I still did not have a date with the hottest guy in school, but anyway, I was going with my three bests friends in the whole world: Melody, Melanie, and Stanley. Stanley's dad owns a limousine company, and he let us borrow one for tonight. I could not believe that I was actually going to ride in a limo; this is so exciting. Stanley is going to pick up Melody and Melanie before me because they live farther away from the school. They are going to pick me up at 5:30 p.m., so I still have a few hours to get ready.

I went to my vanity table to put on some makeup. I put pink on my cheeks, pink on my eyelids, and gloss on my lips. The gloss was clear and sparkly, but it looked nice on me. I didn't want to use too much color on my lips since I already had color on my cheeks and eyelids. But since I used a clear gloss on my lips, I decided to use mascara on my eyelashes to make my eyes pop. When I was done applying makeup, I grabbed my dress from out of my closet and put it on. I stood by my mirror, looking at my dress, trying to decide what would go best with it, and then all of a sudden, my sister pops into my room.

"Oh. Wow! Sis, you look so amazing," said Ashley. "This brings back memories of my high school dances. Let me take a look at you; turn around."

I turned around slowly so she could see my dress.

"Very beautiful! Where did you buy this dress?" she asked.

"I got it at LeAnna's Fashion Boutique; it is a new store in town. The outside doesn't look like much, but the inside of this place is beautiful. This place has so many sparkly things . . . it is like a giant treasure chest. I am glad you like my dress," I told her as I grabbed the sides of my dress and spun around once. I stopped spinning and said, "I did not know you were going to be in town today."

"I told Mom that I was coming, but I didn't want her to tell you," said Ashley. "I wanted to surprise you."

"Well, you surprised me all right," I replied with a laugh.

"Hey, sis," said Ashley. "You have no accessories to go with your dress."

"No, not yet," I said. "I couldn't decide what pieces would go best with my new dress."

"Okay, I will help you find something," said my sister.

She walked over to my jewelry box and looked for the most perfect piece of jewelry that would complement my dress.

"How about these?" Ashley asked as she lifted up sterling silver hoops with pink gems. "These have little pink gems on top. I think these would be a perfect accessory to add to your evening gown."

She brought them over to me so I could see them closer; then, she gently placed them in my ears.

"Those are beautiful," I replied as I looked at my reflection in the mirror. I almost didn't recognize myself. I look so grown up. My sister couldn't have chosen a better pair of earrings. I actually look really pretty.

She smiled and looked at me through the mirror and said, "See, this complements the dress so perfectly. I want to give you one of my favorite necklaces to wear tonight."

She took a necklace out of her shirt pocket and placed it around my neck. It was my favorite diamond-encrusted cross that she used to wear all the time. It used to be my grandmother's, my mom's, then Ashley's, and now mine. It's a family heirloom that has been passed down from generation to generation.

"Your ride is here," yelled my mother.

I glanced out my window and started laughing nervously.

"You have fun tonight," said my sister.

"I will," I replied.

I placed on my pink heels and walked gracefully down the stairs.

"You look so beautiful, honey," said both of my parents.

"No, she looks exquisite," said my sister as she walked behind me down the stairs.

"She has got my mother's necklace on," cried my mom.

My father looked like he had tears in his eyes. "My little princess is all grown up."

I smiled and thanked my family for the wonderful compliments. I gave each one of them a hug and walked out to the limousine.

"Wait!" shouted my mom. "I want to take a picture of you four. I want Cynthia to remember the special day she had with her friends."

"Oh, Mom," I said as I started blushing.

Melody, Melanie, and Stanley all got out of the limo. Melody was wearing a white top and a black skirt. I knew she wouldn't wear a gown like me. Melanie was dressed in a light blue gown with flats. She doesn't like to wear heels. Last but not least, Stanley was wearing a blue tuxedo. He looked very handsome in it, I might add. We all stood together in three different poses: one serious, one of us smiling, and the last one with us being goofy. After we took pictures, Melody, Melanie, and Stanley got back into the limo.

My mom took one more picture of me by myself, then Melody rolled down her window and yelled, "Hey, girl, we have a dance to go to. You have been talking about this dance for months. Let's go; we don't want to be late."

I started to laugh, hugged my family again, and then I saw Mrs. Birkly out in the yard. She was gardening and watering her rose bushes. She seems to be very content as I noticed one of her cats was out in the yard watching her garden. Mrs. Birkly's gaze went from the dirt on the ground to the limousine out on the street. She began to walk across the street.

"Cynthia, you look absolutely beautiful," Mrs. Birkly said. "I see that you are going to a dance with your friends . . . how nice. I remember those days when I went with Mr. Birkly."

Oh my gosh! I almost forgot. I still have Mrs. Birkly's bracelet. "I will be right back." I quickly ran inside and up the stairs. I felt like a princess running away from her prince. I never thought I would sort of reenact my favorite scene from an animated movie I saw when I was a child. The only thing that was missing was my prince.

I went over to my jewelry box and grabbed Mrs. Birkly's bracelet and ran back down the stairs without tripping in my heels. That was a miracle that I didn't trip . . . I could have ripped my gown. I ran past my sister, and she gave me the craziest expression, the one like you do when you have seen a ghost or an unexplained object.

I made it in front of Mrs. Birkly. It felt like the day I saved her from the robber.

"Mrs. Birkly, I have something for you," I said as I reached out my arm and opened my hand almost like it was a flower starting to bloom.

"What is it?" Mrs. Birkly looked in the cup of my hand. "It's my bracelet. You found my bracelet. I never thought I would see this again. Where in the world did you find this?"

I did not want to tell her that the robber snuck it into my jacket, but that's what happened. I didn't really have much time to explain. All I wanted to do was to see a smile on her face. I gently dropped the bracelet in her hand. "I was just lucky to find it . . . I guess."

"Come on," Melody yelled. "We are going to be late."

"I am so grateful to have this back," Mrs. Birkly said as I ran to the limo.

I opened the door to the limo, and I smiled back at Mrs. Birkly. My smile was my way of saying "you're welcome" without words. I am so happy that she finally has her bracelet back. Now, I am ready to go to the dance. I jumped in the limo, and the driver drove down the street.

The dance was exactly like I expected it to be. The blue walls gave the room a romantic feeling of enchantment, with the beautiful array of gems and seashells decorating the walls. On the ceiling, there were circular lights that changed from blue to purple to green every few minutes. The tables were placed all around the dance floor, which was in the center. And the music was jamming so loud that the gymnasium walls were shaking.

My friends and I walked to a table on the left side of the room and sat down. I looked around the room admiring the décor when all of a sudden, I became very hungry. I searched the room once more but no food counter in sight. I was going to wait till we all ate together, but maybe I will ask my friends if they know where the food counter is located.

"Boy, I am starving. Do they have something good for us to eat? Anyway, where is the food counter, by the way?"

Stanley is usually the first one to say he is hungry, but this time it was me.

"I am hungry, too," said Melanie.

We looked around the room, wondering where the staff placed the food table. Then we put our eyes on a beautiful angel ice sculpture. The angel resembled the one we have on the top of our fountain in the front of the school. As we looked past the angel, we found the food table.

"There's the food," said Melody. "Let's go get some."

"How can you guys be so hungry with all of this excitement?" Stanley said. "Plus . . . we ate a ton of cookies in the limo."

I was surprised to hear him say that because he is always hungry.

At that moment, I just let out a short giggle, and then I looked straight at Melody. Melody's expression gave me the impression that she was confused as to why I was laughing. "What's so funny?" Melody asked as her face continued to look confused.

"Nothing," I replied with my notion that it wasn't that important to say out loud. It seems like she doesn't believe me. I guess she really wanted to hear it since she kept on asking me. After about the third time she asked, I finally decided to tell her. "I just thought it was funny that we were hungry and Stanley wasn't. You know how Stanley is; he is always hungry."

"Yes, I am always hungry," said Stanley. "But I am too excited to eat."

Melody, Melanie, and I got up to get a bite to eat when all of a sudden, you know who came into the room. You guessed it. Jason and Brittany walked in like they were already crowned the king and queen of the ball. Everyone stopped dancing and eating to watch them make their entrance. *This is ridiculous*, I thought. I can't believe how much attention those two were getting. Brittany was dressed in a formal red gown holding a sparkly gold clutch, and Jason wore a black tuxedo. Boy, did he look handsome.

Anyway, the DJ started to speak, "Yo! Yo! Yo! This is DJ Spinner. If you would like to hear a particular song, come up and make a request."

After the DJ announcement, one of the chaperones came up to the front of the room and spoke. "Welcome, everyone, to the Beyond the Sea Dance. We have plenty of food, refreshments, and music to enjoy. So, everyone, have fun and enjoy the night." As she was about to walk away, she remembered something. "Oh, we will announce the king and queen in about forty minutes. Have fun, everyone." She walked back to her post in the corner of the room and supervised the students.

The three of us girls went up to the food bar to get something to eat and drink.

At the same time, I heard Brittany ask Jason something. "Jason, sweetie." She stroked Jason's hair and looked at me with a fake smile. "I am feeling a little parched. Can you get me some punch?"

"Sure, sweetie," said Jason. "I will do anything for you."

The sound of that suddenly made me feel a little queasy. I can't believe those two talking to each other like that; so gross. How could Jason talk to her like that after all she has put us through? It's disgusting since I think those two are so wrong for each other, but what can I do? I mean, they are both popular and run the school, so there is really nothing I can do except let them be together. The thought of that made me even more nauseous.

Melanie looked at me and asked, "Are you okay, Cynthia? You look like you are getting sick."

"I am fine, Melanie," I said as I noticed Jason was approaching. I wasn't getting sick, but my stomach felt like it was tied in a knot. Seeing Jason coming in my direction made me even more nervous. What if Jason wanted to talk to me? I couldn't say anything to him with Brittany standing there.

"Oh, I see what's going on . . . secret crush is approaching," said Melody. "We will leave you two alone."

"No!" I yelled at my friends. I quickly started piling food on my plate, trying to be done before he got there, but I was too slow.

I started pouring my punch when he started to talk to me. "You look very pretty tonight, Cindy."

I have never heard him call me Cindy before. Actually, no one has ever called me Cindy before, not even my family. I must have made a strange expression on my face after he called me Cindy because he seemed a little worried.

"Can I call you Cindy?"

"Sure, you can call me Cindy," I replied nervously. "Thanks for the compliment, and you don't look too bad yourself."

I thought it was cute that Jason called me Cindy. I just haven't been used to being called Cindy because everyone usually calls me Cynthia. I started to smile at the thought of having a nickname, especially one from my crush. I was so happy that I have a nickname that I felt like I was floating on cloud nine. Once Jason spoke again, my cloud disappeared, and I went right back to reality.

"Thanks. I got this tuxedo a couple of months ago. I am so sorry that I could not take you to this dance," said Jason in his soft, sincere voice. "Brittany wanted me to come with her, so I couldn't let the princess down."

In my head, I was thinking, *why not?*

"Well, you enjoy yourself tonight," said Jason. "I will talk to you later."

As Jason was about to leave, the angry princess Brittany showed up and stomped her foot. "What is taking so long with the drinks? Oh, it's you. I should have known," she said as she looked at me. Then her angry voice came out. "I thought I told you to stay away from him."

"He came over to have a conversation with me," I replied.

"Oh, did he?" Brittany asked as she gave a mean look to Jason.

"Come on, Brittany, you are being a little paranoid," Jason said, laughing. "It was just a chat between two friends; at least we were not making out."

"Why on earth would you bring up such a thing?" Brittany asked. "I am going to the ladies' room to powder my nose. Come, Mandy and Crystal, I need my girls."

Mandy and Crystal stopped dancing and followed Brittany to the ladies' room.

"I am so sorry about this, Cindy. She gets so jealous when other girls talk to me. I can't help that I am so attractive to the opposite gender," said Jason as he smiled at me. Then he got back to his serious face. "I am going to check on her."

I couldn't believe Jason said that; he really thinks he is so hot. Oh well, it's true.

Stanley was still dancing, so he missed all of the excitement.

"Wow," said Melody. "I can't believe she made a scene about you talking to Jason."

"Yeah, me either," said Melanie. "She is very emotional and sensitive about her man."

"Tell me about it," I said in a sarcastic way.

"What are you going to do now?" asked Melody.

"I am not going to do a thing," I said. "Let's forget about Brittany and have some fun, okay? After all, we are at a dance. I am not going to let Brittany ruin my night."

"Well . . . maybe," said Melanie. "One of us should go and cheer up Brittany."

"Why would we do that?" Melody asked. "That would only make things worse."

"I just thought that it would be the right thing to do," said Melanie.

I hurried up and ate the rest of my food, then Stanley came over. I looked up at him. His hair was still perfectly styled as it was before, but he looked extra cute to me. His face was a little sweaty from all of the dancing he did, and his cheeks were rosy. What? What am I doing? I can't believe I am crushing on my friend Stanley. I mean, he is a good-looking guy, but I never thought I would develop any feelings for him. I am just going to keep these feelings to myself. If Melody and Melanie ever found out about this, they would constantly tease me for the rest of my life.

"You guys haven't danced yet?" Stanley asked.

"No, but we are going to in a bit," said Melanie. "We had more Brittany drama that you missed."

"Aw man . . . I missed the Brittany drama," said Stanley. "I can't believe I missed that, but I was having too much fun dancing."

"Oh, we will tell you about it later," I told him. "Let's dance." I grabbed his arm and pulled him to the dance floor.

"I have never seen you so eager to dance," said Stanley.

"Yeah," I told him. "I am just really excited to dance, that's all."

I moved my feet from side to side, and then Stanley twirled me around.

Meanwhile, in the ladies' room, Brittany was still sobbing. Brittany was sitting in front of a vanity table with her girls sitting by her.

"How could he do this to me, especially on the day of my crowning?" Brittany said with a sob.

"He was just chatting with her," said Crystal.

"You better not be on his side," shouted Brittany. "I could always get another friend to take your place."

"Sorry, Brittany," said Crystal. "I won't say anything more. I don't want to make you more upset."

Then, there was a knock at the door.

"Baby, it's me, Jason. I am sorry. I didn't mean to upset you. Can you please forgive me?"

"Leave me alone, Jason," said Brittany.

Jason gave up and walked away from the door.

"He did say he was sorry," said Mandy. "Why don't you forgive Jason and go dance with him?"

"Yeah, Brittany, you should go dance with him," said Crystal. "I mean, he did take you, not her, to the dance. That should mean something, right? Come on, how many more dances do you get to go to in a lifetime?"

"Well, I guess it is better than staying in here crying," said Brittany.

"In not too long, you will be crowned queen," said Crystal. "Let's fix your makeup."

Mandy got Brittany's makeup bag out of her purse and dumped all of its contents on the counter. Mandy picked up a makeup brush and a pinkish-red eyeshadow and handed them to Crystal. Crystal grabbed the shadow and brush, and then she twisted the eyeshadow lid to open it. Crystal dabbed the brush into the pinkish-red shadow and smeared it across Brittany's eyelids. Mandy picked up a makeup remover cloth and wiped the mascara that smeared from around Brittany's eyes. Mandy then searched for the mascara, and when she found it, she gently reapplied it to Brittany's lashes. Then Crystal swirled a makeup brush into the pink blush and swirled it across the apples of Brittany's cheeks. Next, Crystal applied red lipstick to Brittany's lips and added a clear gloss over the top to make her lips shiny.

"You look beautiful," said Crystal. "Makeup always does the trick. It can hide anything."

"It looks like you haven't cried a bit," said Mandy. "Your face looks awesome."

"Yes, I know," said Brittany. "It always does. I hope it stays that way."

Brittany came out with her makeup looking perfect and smiling as if nothing had happened.

"Come on, sweetie," she said as she grabbed Jason's hand and walked with him to the center of the dance floor. Brittany wrapped her arms around Jason's neck during the slow dance, and she smiled. But she wasn't smiling about dancing with Jason. She had a more perfect scheme in mind. A scheme to make Cynthia's life more miserable.

The fast-paced music suddenly stopped, and a short girl with red hair named Valerie came to the mic in front of us. Everyone was upset about the silence of music, but then they all realized why she was there. It was time to announce the king and queen of the ball.

"I hope everyone is having an awesome night," said Valerie. "I surely am. We have collected and received all of the ballots. Now we are ready to announce the winners."

I already knew who was going to win, but I listened and watched anyway.

"Okay, we are going to do something different this year," said Valerie. "We are going to announce the king first, then the queen." Valerie slowly opened her envelope. "The king of this year's dance is . . . Jason Taylor."

Everyone in the room hollered and screamed as Jason walked up to accept his crown. As I was watching him, he seemed really nervous to me. His body was stiff and tense, and he seemed a little scared. He always walks with confidence every time I have seen him. But this time was different; he seemed insecure, and his confidence was gone. I have never seen him this way before. Why would a popular guy like Jason be nervous? Perhaps he gets embarrassed when the girls scream after they hear his name. Or maybe he doesn't like to be treated like a high-school celebrity.

Maybe I should have screamed, too, but I just didn't feel like it because of the scene that happened earlier. I am kind of giving up hope that Jason and I will be together. I mean, Jason and Brittany are a cute couple; maybe they do belong together. I was starting to cry when they were about to announce the queen. As I glanced up, I noticed Jason was looking at me. At each glance that his eyes met mine, I became more nervous, so I decided to walk to the bathroom. I wanted to look at him, but I just couldn't this time. If I looked at his beautiful blue eyes again, my feelings for him would return. And I couldn't let myself fall for him again since he is with Brittany.

"Okay, this is the moment you all have been waiting for," said Valerie. "The queen is . . . Brittany Woods."

I reached the bathroom door and turned around to hear all of the students screaming for her. I couldn't see her from where I was at, but all I could see was the spotlight in the crowd. The spotlight followed her from the middle of the dance floor to standing beside Jason. The whole crowd screamed as they placed the crown on her shiny blond hair. I know I said I wasn't going to glance at Jason again, but I just couldn't help myself. I looked at him, and he was acting strange. To me, it was like he didn't want to be up there. He kept making repetitive glances between Brittany and me. But what I couldn't decipher was his reason for doing that.

I walked into the bathroom and sat at the vanity table. The tears started falling from my eyes so fast that I couldn't keep my face dry. I wish I wasn't so lovesick. Jason is the only guy I have ever really liked or might even love. *Too bad he didn't have a twin*, I thought, which made me smile. Suddenly, I heard a knock on the door. But who was it? I wasn't sure, but I quickly dried my tears before they came in.

"Cynthia, it's Melody and Melanie. Can we please come in?"

I started to perk up, and I told them, "Yes, you can come in."

"What is the matter?" Melanie asked.

"Oh, I just got upset about the incident that happened earlier,"

I told them. "How I can't even talk to Jason without upsetting Brittany. Or how I will never get a chance to be with him because of a popularity contest."

The tears flowed down my cheeks like a river that flows down a mountain.

"I knew it!" Melody shouted. "I knew it was going to upset you when you saw Jason get crowned. I had a feeling that coming to this dance was a bad idea."

"I am sorry that I am crying. No . . . this wasn't a bad idea. I am glad I came to this dance. I was going to have to face Brittany and Jason eventually. Why not do it here at the dance? I am just having my own Brittany moment," I said as a little smirk appeared on my face.

"It's okay, Cynthia," said Melanie. "We are here for you."

Melody and Melanie both gave me a hug. They told me everything was going to be all right as soon as the dance was over.

I told Melody and Melanie that I had enough excitement for one evening and that I was ready to go home. Melanie and Melody went to search for Stanley so that we could all go home together. In a text message, Melody told me that Stanley wasn't ready to leave, but I knew he would come anyway since he was our ride. I dried up my tears, and I met my friends by the photographer's station.

"I know we are all ready to go home, but how about we take a picture together to capture this moment?"

"Are you sure you want to do this?" Melody asked. "I mean, with all of the excitement you had today."

"Yes, I do," I told them. "It looks like fun. Besides, one day, we might all laugh about this night."

We all went over to the photographer's station, which wasn't busy at the moment. We stood in a row as the photographer snapped our picture.

I never thought in a million years that I would actually go to a dance. I always thought you had to go with a boy, but you can also go with friends. But what was about to happen in just a few minutes was what I thought . . . impossible. As I was about to leave, I heard someone calling my name. I turned around and saw no one. The second time I heard my name being called, I turned around and saw that it was Jason.

"I saw you looking so sad in the audience," said Jason. "I hope you are okay. I wanted to talk to you, but I couldn't get away. I wanted to give you this radio charm to remind you of the dance. I hope you enjoyed this dance as much as I did."

Jason looked around to see if anyone was there watching. He gradually leaned in and kissed me on the lips.

Was I dreaming? Or was this really happening? Who cares? I was having the moment of my life that I have always dreamed about.

CHAPTER ELEVEN

"Why would they do this to me?" I asked Melody and Melanie the next morning at school.

"I don't know," said Melanie.

"The photographers just wanted to pick on somebody to give themselves a laugh," said Melody.

"Well . . . I don't think this is funny," I said as I walked around looking at the dozens of pictures on the wall of Jason and me kissing. "I don't know how the photographers got us on camera because when the kiss happened, there were no photographers in sight."

Then Melanie spoke. "Maybe someone set up a security camera and recorded everything, then took a picture of you and Jason kissing while they watched the video."

"Yeah, I have seen things like that happen before," said Melody. "I hope they did not do that to you, Cynthia."

"How could someone be so mean and ruin a moment of happiness?"

As soon as I said that, I looked up and noticed Brittany standing a few feet away from me with her hands on her hips. When I saw her, I knew right then and there that she set me up somehow.

"You did it!" I shouted as I pointed at Brittany.

Brittany walked closer to me and said, "How do you like your pictures around the school? Don't you and Jason make such a cute couple?" Brittany asked in a sarcastic voice.

Before I got to respond to that question, Brittany let out a big, "Uh . . . no!"

"Why you?" Melody shouted as she was ready to punch Brittany out.

"No, Melody," Melanie said as she grabbed Melody's arm to hold her back from beating Brittany up.

"Why not?" Melody asked.

"Physical violence is not the answer," said Melanie. "We should be able to talk this out like mature adults."

"Yeah, you are right," said Melody.

"Brittany, how could you do this to me?" I asked. "I thought we would be more mature than this. If you have a problem with me, tell me about it first, instead of doing something crazy like this. Please stop thinking of a way to get me back from something I did that upset you."

"I guess you are right," said Brittany. "We are all mature adults here. I do not like that you secretly talk to Jason when I am not around. Plus, I saw you kissing him at the dance."

"I did not kiss him; he kissed me first," I shouted.

"Why don't I believe you, then?" Brittany said with her hands on her hips. "Like I said when I first met you, just stay away from him. Am I clear, Cynthia?"

She had this awful mean look in her eyes that I have never seen before. To tell you the truth, that was the look I never wanted to see again.

"Yes, you are clear," I said with a frightened look on my face.

She flipped her hair and walked down the hall as if nothing had happened as her cheerleader posse followed right behind her.

"Why do you let her talk to you like that?" Melody asked. "If it were me, I would give her a piece of my mind."

"No, if I did that, then it would make this situation a lot worse," I said. "I can't stoop to her level. I have tried reasoning with her, but that didn't work either. I don't know what to do to make her stop picking on me."

"Come on, Cynthia; enough talk about Brittany," said Melody. "Let's get to class."

"We will worry about her later," said Melanie.

While I walked to class, I searched for Jason to see if he knew anything about the disaster that happened ten minutes ago. I looked, and looked, and looked, but he was nowhere in sight. I asked a few students if they knew where Jason was, and they all replied with a slight giggle and a harsh no. As I reached closer to my Spanish class, I found a guy standing right next to two exit doors at the end of the hallway. This guy was about five-foot-nine with brown hair and green eyes. His name was Ryan, as I could tell by the name tag that he was wearing.

"Hi, Ryan. I am sorry to bother you. I am Cynthia Adams. I wanted to know if you have seen Jason Taylor?"

"Yeah, I have seen him," said Ryan. "He was in auto shop today, but he left early because of the photos. He felt so bad about what happened that he could not stay at school. He knew you would be looking for him, so he told me to tell you that he was sorry. He said he would try to make it up to you somehow."

"Do you know where I could find him?" I asked. "I need to talk to him."

"No, sorry, I do not," said Ryan. "Jason is kind of secretive when it comes to where he goes to hang out. I guess he does that to get away from his girlfriend."

"Well, thanks, Ryan," I said. "You were a lot of help."

"You're welcome, Cynthia," said Ryan. "Anytime."

After Spanish class was over, it was lunch time. Except, I did not head to lunch. I went searching for Jason to see if he was still at school. I really had to talk to him to see if he knew anything about the photos. After about fifteen minutes of searching, I finally found him. He was outside in front of the school, standing by the fountain. Jason did not seem like his outgoing, popular self. He looked sad and heartbroken—an image of Jason I have never seen till now. I wish I could have done something to cheer him up, but what could I do? I couldn't make anything worse, so I just decided to approach him.

"Hey, Jason. I have been searching all over for you," I said. "Where have you been?"

"Oh please, Cynthia, don't come near me," Jason replied. "I have already caused you enough trouble."

"Why? Are you sick?"

"No, I am not sick," Jason replied with a confused look on his face.

"Then, why can't I talk to you?"

"I don't want you to get hurt," said Jason. "You are one of my true friends who knows who I really am. I can't bear to see you get hurt again. There is no telling what Brittany will do next."

"Why are you letting Brittany make your life miserable?"

"She forced me to date her because we are the two most popular students in the school. And if I tried to leave her, she told me that she would find a way to kick me off the football team," said Jason as tears flowed down his face. "I don't want to be kicked off the team because it gives me joy and happiness when I play. If I lose football and Brittany, I will be . . . . nobody."

"That's not true," I told him. "You are not a nobody. You are just trying to find yourself . . . like the rest of us. I would not put up with Brittany. If I were you, I would stand up to her."

Gosh, I am beginning to sound like Melody.

"I will try someday, maybe sometime in the future," said Jason.

"I hope that the future is not too far away."

"I hope not either. Maybe we can give Brittany some of her own medicine," said Jason with a slight grin on his face.

CHAPTER TWELVE

I sat and wondered what Jason had planned to do to stand up to Brittany. I don't know why he does everything that Brittany asks of him. I mean, that's good in a way that he is a gentleman, but why does he mind her? She is so unkind. I think Jason might be afraid to stand up to her because he doesn't want to lose his popularity and friends. But actually, he won't lose his true friends because they will stick by him, no matter what happens.

I have wanted to talk to Jason since I last saw him, but I have not seen him for weeks. Where has he gone? The photo of us that Brittany put up in the school hallway must have really hurt him. I have never seen him like this. I hope he is doing okay.

We have about a month left until summer vacation. I can't wait to escape from all of this drama until school starts back up again in the fall. Melody, Melanie, Stanley, and I will be sophomores. Brittany and Jason will be juniors.

I am so glad today is Friday. It has been two weeks since the dance and photo craziness. I still haven't heard from Jason. Today is the last football game of the season, so I am going to try to get Stanley, Melanie, and Melody to come with me. I hope I get to talk to Jason sometime today, if I see him.

I am sitting here in my science class waiting for the bell to ring for lunch. I haven't heard anything more about our kissing photo; it must be old news by now. I am sitting here thinking of all these things while watching Brittany send text messages while applying on makeup at the same time. It is kind of fascinating. I don't know how she does both at the same time.

I have a little urge inside me that wants to talk to Brittany. I know, it sounds crazy, but I want to find out if she knows where Jason is, but then again, she probably wouldn't tell me if she knew, anyway. I started to get up from my chair, and then I sat back down again. I said a quiet "no" out loud that nobody else heard except for me. I am going to talk to her if it is the last thing I do. I walked over to Brittany and stood in front of her desk as I watched her file her bright, shiny red nails.

Brittany glanced up from filing her nails. "What do you want, Cynthia? Can't you see I am busy?"

"I know you are busy, but can I ask you a question?"

"Sure, I guess . . . but you will just be wasting my beauty care regimen time," said Brittany.

I just rolled my eyes in disgust. She has got to be kidding, right? So, I started to speak anyway. "Um . . . Brittany, have you seen Jason lately? I haven't seen him for a few weeks now."

Brittany started to get this annoyed look on her face, and then she began to laugh. "Why would I tell you where he is? He doesn't even like you, Cynthia. He told me personally that he doesn't like you anymore, and he never wants to see you again."

"Did he really say that, Brittany?"

"Ah, yeah, he did," Brittany replied.

My heart started pounding rapidly like the drums in the school band. I don't know if she was telling the truth or not, but I was deeply hurt by it.

It was finally lunch time, and I started walking slowly to the cafeteria.

Melody, Melanie, and Stanley were already at their table waiting for Cynthia to arrive.

"Where is she?" Melody asked. "She should have been here by now."

"I hope she is okay," said Melanie. "She has been having a rough time since the dance."

"She has gone through worse things than the dance," Stanley added. "She will be fine."

"Look, there she is," said Melanie.

"Why is she walking so slow?" Melody asked.

"It looks like she is having another bad day," added Stanley.

I did not want my friends to notice how slow I was walking, so I started to walk faster, but I wasn't quick enough; they already saw me before I got to the table.

"Why are you walking so slow?" Melody asked.

"Did someone hurt you?" Melanie asked.

Stanley just stayed out of the conversation and continued to eat his lunch.

"Sorry, guys, I didn't mean to get you guys upset," I said. "The whole day was going great until the end of science class."

Stanley seemed to be more interested in his meal until I mentioned the words "end of science class." His eyes became bright and attentive, and he started to join in on our conversation. "What happened in science class that made you so gloomy?"

"Well, you guys aren't going to like this, but I had this urge to talk to Brittany about Jason."

"Why on earth would you do that, Cynthia?" Melody shouted. "I thought our main focus was to stay away from her. You know how much Brittany dislikes us."

"I know, but I have been worried," I said. "It's not like Jason to be gone this long."

"Did you get anything out of her?" Melanie asked.

"No, I apparently did not. She was very snotty, and she laughed when I asked about Jason. The snotty remarks and laughing didn't bother me so much. But, when she said that Jason didn't like me anymore and that he never wanted to see me again, it broke my heart."

"Aw . . . Cynthia," said Melanie. "She should not have said that to you."

"She is probably lying to you like she always does," added Melody.

"Well, Jason did say earlier that he didn't want me to come near him, so maybe it's true."

"Yes, he did say that, but he also said he didn't want you to get hurt," Melanie added. "So, that shows he does care about you."

"Cynthia, don't worry about it," said Melody. "She is just lying to you to make you more miserable."

"I try not to worry about it, but it's hard sometimes," I said. "Well, for some reason, I think she is telling the truth, but at other times, I think she is lying. I know the true Jason cares about me, but the true Jason hardly ever comes out when Brittany is around. The one question I would like to have answered is, why is this happening to me?"

"I don't know why this is happening to you, but I am going to find out," said Stanley as he picked up his tray and walked away.

CHAPTER THIRTEEN

I have invited my friends Melanie and Melody over to watch a movie before the Friday night football game. While the previews were playing, I quietly asked Melody and Melanie if they have seen Stanley. It has been nearly two hours, and I haven't heard from him. Melody was lying on her stomach, throwing popcorn in her mouth while watching the movie.

"No, Cynthia," said Melody. "I haven't seen or heard from Stanley since lunch time."

"How about you, Melanie?" I asked.

"No, I haven't heard from him, either," said Melanie as she accidentally dropped a piece of popcorn on the couch.

"I hope he shows up soon. It's not like him not to call."

"Don't worry about it; he will show up," Melody said in a frustrated tone. "Let's watch the movie."

I grabbed some popcorn from the bowl on the coffee table and sat on the floor next to Melody. The movie began, and it started to tell us a story about a princess who is trapped in a castle who needs to be rescued by her one true love.

"I just love watching fairy tale movies," I said as I threw a piece of popcorn in my mouth. "They are so romantic."

Meanwhile, while the girls were watching their movie, Stanley was out looking for answers. Stanley hung around the gym and waited patiently for Brittany to get out of cheerleading practice.

"Good job, girls. Nicely done," said Brittany. "I think you are all ready for the big game tonight. Go, team." Brittany raised her right arm in the air, then she jumped up and did a split in the air. As she came down, she landed back on her feet. Afterward, she decided to walk out of the gym for a moment. Brittany turned to the left of the gymnasium door and bent down to drink some water out of the fountain. She straightened up, turned around, and saw Stanley sitting on the bench.

"Um, do you want something?" Brittany asked.

"Yes, actually, I want to talk to you," Stanley replied. "You really hurt my friend's feelings this morning, and all I want are some answers. She was just really worried about her friend, and she just wanted to know if he was okay, that's all. Cynthia is a caring person; you didn't have to be so mean to her."

"I wasn't mean to her. I was just telling her the truth," Brittany said as she fluffed her hair. "I guess your little friend can't handle the truth."

"But, that wasn't the truth; you lied to her," said Stanley. "You told her that Jason didn't like her and never wanted to see her again."

"Yeah, I did tell her that, didn't I?" Brittany said as she moved her arm to glance at her red nails. "Well, that's what she gets for wanting to date a guy that already loves me."

"By what she tells me, I don't think he loves you, Brittany," said Stanley. "I don't think you two are really dating, either. I think it's more of a popularity act than anything else."

"Yeah . . . you are probably right," said Brittany in a snotty tone. "But it's really none of your business, by the way."

"Oh, excuse me for caring about my friend," said Stanley. "Now, I have one more question. Where is Jason?"

"If I answer this, will you be on your way?" Brittany said. "I still have a lot of cheers to practice."

"Yes, I will leave you alone," said Stanley.

"Okay, I think Jason is hiding out under the bleachers," said Brittany. "That's where he usually hangs out when he wants to be alone."

"Thanks, Brittany," said Stanley.

"No need to thank me," she said as she walked back into the gym while rolling her eyes.

Stanley walked to the football stadium, which was just outside the door near the gym. The bleachers were empty, and the sky looked like it was going to rain. Stanley kept looking under the bleachers until he finally found Jason. Jason was sitting on a wooden bench staring at the wall. He looked really depressed from Stanley's viewpoint, but all Stanley could see was Jason's back and his shadow on the ground. Stanley did not know exactly what to say to him since he has never had a real conversation with Jason, but he tried to act as cool as possible in front of him.

"Hey, Jason," said Stanley as he turned on the light. "I have been looking all over for you, man."

"You have? I have been under here all day," said Jason as he turned around to face Stanley. "I don't want to face the people at school today."

"Why not?" Stanley asked. "You are the most popular dude in school."

"Yeah, I know, but being popular isn't who I really am," said Jason. "I am a little tired of being popular. I don't want to feel like I have to be popular to be liked by others."

"Wow, dude! You are getting really deep here," said Stanley. "You sound like Cynthia. You have one thing in common with her;

she likes to have deep conversations too. Oh boy, going deep is not my thing."

"How is Cynthia?" Jason asked. "I feel so bad that I hurt her. She probably doesn't want to see me anymore, does she?"

"Now, that's strange," said Stanley. "Cynthia heard from Brittany that you didn't want to see her again."

"Well, apparently, Brittany lied to both of us. I actually do want to see her again," said Jason as he looked down at his untied shoelace. "I just don't want Brittany to hurt her again, so I am just staying away from everyone; then no one gets hurt."

"Jason, it's not your fault," said Stanley. "Brittany is the one to blame here, not you. Staying away from Cynthia is not the best way to help her. If you stay away from your friends, that tells Brittany she has won. But dude, do what you want."

"What is the best way, then?" Jason asked.

"I think it would be best to talk to Cynthia about it, but I don't want to tell you what to do," said Stanley. Then Stanley thought about changing the subject since having a deep conversation with someone is not really his thing. "Jason, are you going to play in tonight's game?"

Jason perked up and spoke, "Yes, the team can't win without me."

A storm was in progress, and it rained, rained, and rained. Melody, Melanie, and I were finishing up the movie as the prince was fighting the fire-breathing dragon. All of a sudden, lightning struck, and the doorbell rang at the same time. All of us jumped and were frightened.

"I wonder who that could be?" Melanie asked as Cynthia approached the door. "It is too scary and dangerous to be outside in this weather. Ah, and the lightning is so loud and creepy. It makes me jump every time."

"Yeah, I know what you mean, sis," said Melody. "It makes me jump, too, especially when it comes and you're not expecting it."

"Oh, I hate that," I said as I reached the door. "I hope this individual is not a salesperson. I am about broke." I looked through the peephole and saw a young man, but I actually couldn't really tell who he was since it was raining. To get a closer look, I opened the door a tad.

"It is Stanley!" I replied as I opened the door all the way to let him in.

Stanley rushed in like a cheetah running in the wild.

"You are all wet, Stanley," I said. "Do you want some hot chocolate?"

"No, thank you, Cynthia," said Stanley. "Sorry, it took me a while, but I finally got some answers. I found out that Jason and Brittany are not really dating; it's more of a popularity contest for the dance. Jason was told the same thing by Brittany—that you didn't want to see him again. Which is wrong; he really does want to see you."

A smile appeared on my face when he said that.

Stanley continued talking as he saw that I was happy with the news. "Jason is just staying away from everyone because he doesn't want to hurt you again, Cynthia." Stanley looked directly at me. "You should see him, Cynthia; he is really down in the dumps."

"I know he is. Is Jason going to be playing in the game?"

"Yeah, I asked him that after we talked," said Stanley. "He really perked up when I mentioned football. He said that the team couldn't win without him."

"He is so cute when he says stuff like that."

"Oh, brother," said Stanley.

"That's funny," said Melody. "It sounds like Jason is back to his normal self."

"Well, our movie is almost over," I said. "Are we all going to the game together?"

"All three of us girls are going," said Melanie. "I am sure that Cynthia is going just to see you-know-who."

Then I spoke up, "Stop, Melanie, you are embarrassing me." I began to laugh as I looked at Stanley. "Are you coming with us, Stanley?"

"Yes, I need a hot dog right now," said Stanley. "I am really hungry from all of this running around. And Cynthia is buying me dinner."

"Oh, Stanley," said all of the girls together as we laughed out the door.

CHAPTER FOURTEEN

The Bluesville Angels won against the Red Water Dragons with a score of thirteen to seven. It was an amazing victory and the last game of the season. I was sad that I would not be able to see Jason play till next year. But, oh well, I might see him later if he comes. Oh! I did not tell you that Brittany is having an end-of-the-school-year/football party at her house. She invited everyone, even me, which is really odd. Stanley isn't coming because he is at home sick with a cold. Melanie, Melody, and I are all going together.

"Poor Stanley," said Melody. "I wish he could have come. This party isn't going to be any fun without him."

"Yeah . . . if he wouldn't have looked for Jason in the rain, he wouldn't be sick right now."

"He just wanted to make you happy," said Melanie.

"Yes, I know. Stanley is such a great friend. You are all great friends to me," I told them as we hugged. "How about we all go and visit him for a while before we go to the party? We have about an hour before the party starts. And even if we are late, it doesn't matter because we will be spending time with a friend that needs us."

Stanley's house was a street behind mine, so it was easy to walk to. We arrived at his house, and next to the large maple tree was a tomato garden. Melody and Melanie thought we were at the wrong house when they saw the tomato garden, but I knew we were at the right place because Stanley's house is the only one in the neighborhood that has a large maple tree in the front yard. We walked up the steps and knocked at the door. His mom came to the door wearing an apron over a blue and white checkered dress with her curled hair laying over her shoulders.

"Hello, Cynthia, Melody, and Melanie," Stanley's mom said as she looked at each of us. "What can I do for you today?"

She spoke to us like she was still working behind a customer service counter. Stanley always teases his mom when she speaks like this to him, his father, or other people. Stanley used to tell us in middle school that for the fourteen years his mom used to work behind a customer service counter, she hasn't been able to stop talking like that. He thinks it's cute that his mom talks this way; he says it's her way of showing how much she cares about everyone.

I smiled and looked up at Stanley's mom. "Can we come in to see Stanley? We brought him chicken soup and a sports magazine."

"Sure. That was sweet of you," said Stanley's mom. "Come on in. Stanley's room is down the hall and to the right."

His bedroom door was open. Stanley was lying there reading, and he looked so pale.

He glanced up from his book, and he seemed shocked to see us. "Oh . . . hi guys. I did not know you were here. What's up?"

"We wanted to bring you some chicken soup," said Melanie.

"And we also have a sports magazine for you to enjoy," said Melody.

I was about to open my mouth to say something, but Stanley beat me to it. "This soup smells amazing. I am going to eat some now. I am starving."

All I could do was smile as I watched him eat.

Stanley ate another spoonful of soup, and then he placed his soup bowl to the side. He picked up his magazine and stared at the cover. "Oh, cool! My favorite magazine. I did not know this issue was even out yet. I can't wait to read this one. You guys shouldn't have, but I am glad you did."

We all laughed at him. There is the funny Stanley we all know and love.

"Stanley, I am so glad that you helped me with the situation I had with Brittany and Jason," I said. "I want you to know that I really appreciate all of your help. I don't know what I would have done if you didn't step in to help."

"No problem, Cynthia," said Stanley as he grabbed his bowl and placed it on his lap. "That's what friends are for—to help one another through the good and bad times."

"I am just really sad."

"What are you sad about?" Stanley asked as he scooped up some soup and put some in his mouth.

"I am sad that you became sick after you helped me with my situation," I said as my eyes became teary. "And if I would have just kept my mouth shut, you would be healthy and able to go to the party tonight."

"Oh, Cynthia," said Stanley. "Please don't cry. There is nothing to be sad about. I just have a bad cold. I probably would have gotten a cold anyway because I like to be outside. And besides, I was not really interested in going to the party, anyway. I'd rather stay home."

I started to feel a little better, but it felt weird going somewhere without Stanley. He is always with us.

"You guys have fun," Stanley said. "I don't want you to be late. And besides, I will see you guys when you come back."

"We won't be late," said Melanie.

"Bye, Stanley," we said together.

"Bye, girls," said Stanley. "I will be healthy in no time."

Stanley went back to eating his soup, and he began to read his magazine as soon as we left his room.

Back at our house, my mom was waiting for us to return, so she could give us a ride to the party.

"Are you ready, girls?" she asked as she put our bags in the trunk.

"Yes, we went to check on Stanley to see how he was doing."

"How is he doing?" my mom asked.

"He is getting back to his normal self," I said. "He will be better in no time."

"That's good to hear," said my mom. "Girls, you better get into the car. It's time to go. Let's not be late."

Brittany's house was about a fifteen-minute drive from our house. Brittany lives in the most hottest spot in Bluesville, which is our finest Blueswater Beach. It would be awesome to live here. You can swim in the water or walk on the sand anytime you want, have the sun touch your skin with a warming sensation that makes you feel relaxed, and plus, you get tan in the process.

We arrived, hearing the sound of blasting music. It was so loud that I couldn't hear anyone talk. My mom walked out of the car, covering her ears while she got our bags out of the trunk.

"How can anyone hear anything in this place? So much noise and no peace and quiet. Girls, are you sure you want to stay here?" As she was talking, a couple of surfer guys with their boards ran past her, almost knocking her over. "See what I mean, girls? These guys are wild, and they have no sense of manners."

As soon as she finished her last sentence, one of the surfer guys came up to my mom. "Sorry, ma'am. I didn't mean to almost knock you down. My brother and I are in a real rush, man. These waves are rising high. Oh! Excuse me. I forgot to introduce myself." He smiled at the girls, and then he looked at his brother. "My name is Cameron, and this is my brother Anthony. Well, it was really nice to meet everyone. I am going to catch some waves with my bro."

"It was nice meeting both of you," said my mom.

We watched them leave, and I thought they were both so good-looking. Looking at them made me forget about Jason.

Melody looked at me and whispered in my ear. "I think Cameron is so hot. I want to go talk to him."

My mom saw us looking at the two handsome boys, and she cleared her throat. "Um, earth to girls. Cynthia, focus. You are not here to stare at boys; you are here for the party."

I gave her a funny look, and then I smiled as I remembered that I loved Jason and no one else. But then I thought, *why couldn't I look at boys? Jason and I are not dating yet.*

Melody, Melanie, and I grabbed our bags and started walking around. There were girls laying on towels sun-tanning, guys in swim trunks playing volleyball, people dancing, and guys and girls surfing in the ocean.

"Well, girls, we are finally here," I said excitedly. "What would you guys like to do first?"

"Well . . . " said Melody as she smiled at me and looked directly at the water. "I am going to watch the surfers."

I had a feeling she was going over to flirt with Cameron.

"I am going to stay with you, Cynthia," said Melanie.

Melanie and I stood there watching all the events take place, and all of a sudden, a beach ball was coming toward our heads. I thought, *oh no, not again.* I have a terrible fright against balls ever since the incident in the gym.

"Watch out, girls," a young guy yelled as the ball was approaching our heads. I tried to grab the ball, but I fell flat on my bottom. Then, I heard the young guy fussing at a guy named Ryan for hitting the ball too hard.

"Sorry, man," Ryan yelled as his friend approached me while I was still sitting in the sand.

"Sorry about that, beautiful. My friend here doesn't know how to hit the ball right. May I help you up?" the young guy asked.

"Sure, I would like that," I said as I was glancing toward the sand.

He held out his hand, pulled me up, and I smiled at him. I couldn't believe who it was—of all the people I would run into at the beach. I was so shocked.

"Hey, it's you," we both said at the same time.

"Cynthia, I didn't know you were going to be here."

"I didn't know you were going to be here, either," I added.

"I have been wanting to talk to you, but I didn't think you wanted to see me again," said Jason.

"I do want to talk to you," I told Jason. "I thought you did not want to see me again."

"Whatever you heard wasn't true," said Jason. "I wanted to say that I am sorry that I haven't been around lately. I haven't been in a really good mood. Since you are here, would you like to grab a bite to eat later?"

"Sure, I would like that very much."

I heard a young girl shout in the distance. "Jason, are you coming? Or what? We need the ball back."

Then I realized who it was—Brittany, of all people.

"You're here with her?" I asked.

"Yeah, I am, but she will let me talk to you now since an unknown guy fussed at her," said Jason. "I wish I knew who was brave enough to stand up to her, but she wouldn't say. I would have liked to have known his name. I guess I will never know. But even if this person didn't talk to her, I would have still tried to find a way to talk to you. I am not going to let her stop me from talking to my friends."

I immediately knew he was talking about Stanley. I really did admire Jason's perseverance, though. I really wish I could have told him it was Stanley, but I just couldn't.

"Well, I better get back to my game," said Jason. "See you later, okay?"

He picked up the ball and ran back to the volleyball net. As I was watching Jason leave, Melanie came from out of nowhere.

"I heard him call you 'beautiful,'" said Melanie. "How romantic."

"Yeah, he did, but he said it to me before he knew who I was."

"Come on, girl. Don't deny it," said Melody. "I even heard it, and

I was all the way over there by the surfers."

"How did you hear it?" I asked. "You were all the way over there."

"I have super sensitive ears," said Melody. "I hear everything."

"It's true; we have another name for her ears," said Melanie. "They are supersonic. If there is the slightest pen drop, my sister will hear it."

"Yeah, they must be to be able to hear my conversation."

These two are so funny. In a way, it's like Melody has a superpower. It would be cool to have some sort of superpower like that. When I spend time with two of my best friends, I never know what will come out of their mouths. They are always full of surprises. I began to think of the surprise of being able to see Jason again, and the comment Melody and Melanie made about hearing Jason calling me beautiful. I just had trouble believing that Jason actually thought I was beautiful. To tell you the truth, I actually believed he saw someone else instead of me.

"He probably thought I was an unknown beauty that he hasn't met before."

"Yeah, sure," said Melody. "Whatever you say, Cynthia."

"It's probably true," I told her. "But, I don't want to get down in the dumps talking about him. What are we waiting for? Let's have some fun."

Melody, Melanie, and I walked around the beach for about an hour. I felt so exhausted, and my friends appeared to be, too. All of this walking around sure was making me hungry, but I couldn't see any food counter in sight from where I was standing. Maybe if I wait a few minutes or two, one of my friends will want to eat. I didn't want to eat without them if they weren't hungry. It's just something we do; we always eat together.

"You know what?" said Melody. "All of this walking around is making me hungry."

"I am hungry, too," said Melanie.

"I am sure they have food around here somewhere," I added. "I just don't know where exactly, but we will find it."

We walked around for a few minutes until we found a tent. "This must be it," I hollered as I showed my friends. We walked in as the tent's drapery brushed against our backs, and inside was a nice-sized room with a little buffet counter in front of six picnic tables. As I walked by the counter, I noticed they had barbecue, hot dogs, hamburgers, and all of the sides you could think of, all in one place. I waited at one of the picnic tables in the front row while my friends got their dinner. Suddenly, I spotted Brittany entering the tent with Jason behind her. I noticed Brittany's hair was flat-ironed straight with no hair out of place. And her swimsuit was navy blue with white polka dots. Next, I looked at Jason. His hair was spiked in front after being in the water. His body was tanned, and he was wearing green swim trunks. I haven't noticed before, but Jason has big muscles. Melody and Melanie sat in front of me, and they placed their trays on the table.

"I just noticed that Jason is really fit," I declared.

Then Melody spoke in a snotty tone, and she moved her body in a certain way that covered my view of Jason. "Of course, he's fit. He is a football player, remember?"

"I know he is a football player."

"Oh, I am sorry," said Melody. "I did not mean to say it that way. I get cranky when I am hungry."

"It's okay," I replied. "It's just hard to tell if a guy has muscles or not because of the padding and all."

I went up to the buffet and got a hot dog, some macaroni, and a soda, and then I sat back down.

"I can't get over how awesome this party is," said Melody. "Guess what, Cynthia?"

Melody was so excited that I didn't even have a chance to guess.

"You know that guy I met today?" Melody said with excitement. "You know, Cameron? He asked me out."

"Really? That's wonderful," I squealed. "I am so happy for you."

"I know. I never thought I would meet someone at a party that Brittany organized," said Melody. She switched her gaze from me to Melanie. "Now, Cynthia and my dear sister, I will have to set you both up."

"Oh, come on, Melody," I said. "I don't want to be set up. I get too nervous around guys."

"Look . . . and here comes a potential . . . candidate right now," said Melody teasingly.

"Who gets nervous?" Jason asked as he sat down in front of me. "And what is this talk about candidates?"

"Oh, the candidate thing," said Melanie as she was trying to hold in her laugh. "Melody was just wondering if you, um, were running for class president in the fall."

"Um, no, I probably will not," said Jason. "Running for class president isn't really my thing."

"Good to know," said Melody as she was trying not to laugh. "We wouldn't want you to do something you didn't want to do."

Nice save, Melanie. I didn't think Jason would fall for her story, but he did. I can't believe Melody teased me like that. I am so glad that Jason didn't hear what Melody said. I would have been more nervous than I am now. It was funny, though, watching Melody and Melanie covering up their story while try-ing not to laugh. I didn't think they could hold it in much longer; both of them looked like they were going to burst. I still haven't answered Jason's question. Should I? Or shouldn't I? That's the mere question. I just don't know if I have the guts to admit that I am nervous. But I guess I will have to admit it. I mean, I do have to take some kind of risk in life, even if it means that I am a nervous wreck when it comes to talking with boys.

"I do. I am the one who gets nervous," I told him.

"You don't appear to be nervous when you talk to me," added Jason.

"I know . . . but I try to hide it, so you won't notice," I said, smiling.

"Well, you hide it well," he said with a laugh as he was about to take a bite of his hamburger.

The sun was slowly disappearing, and the moon was shining bright in the night sky. A gentle breeze came through the opened tent and blew my hair to the side. Jason had his eyes fixed on me at that moment, and I was so nervous that I didn't know what to do.

Jason grabbed my hand and said, "I want to show you something."

We both stood up and ran out near the water. Jason pointed up in the sky and showed me the stars.

"Aren't they beautiful?" Jason asked as he looked at me and grabbed my hand to hold.

"Yes, they are beautiful, Jason," I said as I held his hand as I gazed into his beautiful blue eyes.

We stood there, gazing up at the stars. The stars looked like tiny diamonds sparkling in the night sky. How could this moment get any more romantic?

CHAPTER FIFTEEN

Gazing at the stars was so magical. I never thought I would do anything so romantic, especially with my crush. I am sad to see that the summer is ending. In a few days, school will be starting, with the dreaded early mornings and tons of homework. This year, I will be a sophomore. I hope my sophomore year goes better than my freshman year.

On my day back as a sophomore, my year was starting out right.

"I can't believe the night you had," Melanie sighed in a dreamy way. "Gazing at the stars with your one true love. How lovely."

"Melanie, he is not my true love . . . yet." I started to giggle while questioning the thought of Jason being my one true love. It would be a dream come true for me, but it sounds impossible since he is still with Brittany. But anyway, it was a nice thought while it lasted. I looked back at Melanie and smiled. "To have a true love, the other person has to love you . . ."

"It's about time you and Jason had a special moment together," interrupted Melody. "That Brittany has been ruining the relationship you two have had since you both first met."

"Isn't that the truth," I spoke sarcastically.

"Oh, Cynthia," said Melanie as she handed me an envelope. "I almost forgot to give you this."

I took the envelope from her hand and opened it. It was a picture of Jason and I holding hands as we were gazing up at the stars.

"I hope you like it, Cynthia," said Melanie. "I thought you might want to treasure the moment, so I took a picture of you two."

"Like it? I love it! Thank you so much for this beautiful picture, Melanie. I will definitely treasure this moment forever."

"Treasure what moment?" a girl asked from behind me.

"It's none of your business," I declared. "And plus, I don't know who you are, anyway."

Just as I said that I should have known who I was talking to. I was just so caught up in the moment of romance that I was not thinking clearly.

"Oh, I think you know who I am," said Brittany. "I can't believe you actually had a romantic moment with someone. He must be a real loser if he goes out with you."

I don't know why she doesn't think a cute guy would be in a relationship with me. Why is it so impossible for her to believe? A single tear started to fall from my eye.

Suddenly, Melody became really angry and stood up, facing Brittany. Brittany and Melody gave each other a nasty look.

"Brittany," said Melody, "just because you are a year older than us and a junior does not make it right for you to pick on my best friend."

"Well, I would not pick on you guys if your friend would stay away from my boyfriend," said Brittany.

"Really, Brittany?" Melody said with a disgusted look on her face. "Are we discussing this again? I thought we were over this conversation. I heard you guys were not dating, anyway."

Brittany got upset and fluffed her hair back. "I have no idea what you are talking about. I think you are lying."

"Come on, Brittany," said Melody. "I hear more gossip about you two than I hear from my own relatives. I just heard that the two of you were only dating to win the popularity contests."

"Uh . . . where did you hear this nonsense?" Brittany asked. "It is so, like, not true."

"I only hear the truth about you from other people, but not

from you," said Melody. "I guess you just can't handle the truth. Can you, Brittany?"

I looked up, focusing my attention elsewhere. I just had to find a way to distract myself from this situation. My knees were trembling, and I was sweating like crazy. Everyone in the cafeteria was staring at them. I just had a sense that something was going to go wrong, but I just didn't know what might happen. I was scared that Melody would get hurt.

Out of nowhere, Brittany grabbed my envelope from my hand. I did not see that one coming.

I jumped out of my seat and shouted, "Hey, that's mine! Give that back to me!"

"I just wanted to take a look at it," said Brittany, as if she had done nothing wrong.

Melody was about to throw a fist punch at Brittany when Jason showed up to the rescue.

"What is going on here?" Jason demanded.

"I was just having a friendly conversation with my new friends," Brittany said with a fake smile.

Oh, please. I can't believe Brittany actually said that we are her new friends. I hope Jason doesn't fall for it because I sure don't. I moved my gaze from Brittany to Jason. From the expression on his face, I think Jason knew that Brittany was lying to him. As everyone knows, Brittany lies to everybody.

"What do you have in your hand?" Jason asked.

"Oh, just something Cynthia wanted me to see," said Brittany innocently.

Melody and I were both furious as we placed our hands on our hips.

Jason looked at both of us, then he said, "I don't think she wanted you to see this. I think you took it from them."

"Me!" Brittany was flabbergasted. "I would never do such a

thing as to take something that wasn't mine. How dare you say such a thing about your sweet and innocent girlfriend!"

Jason grabbed the envelope from Brittany. "I don't believe you, Brittany. Your so-called new friends' faces say it otherwise. You lied to me too much already. Why should I believe you?"

"Oh my gosh." Brittany was dumbfounded. "I can't believe this; my own boyfriend doesn't trust me. What is the world coming to? Are the freaks taking over the school? Why is this happening to me? What am I going . . . "

As Brittany was rambling on about the freaks taking over the school, I was keeping an eye on Jason. I was hoping that he would not open the envelope. I don't know what I would do if he saw that picture. Oh my gosh, I would be so embarrassed. I might not be able to face Jason again. I have to get the envelope back into my possession somehow.

He gave the envelope back to me and said, "Sorry about this, girls. I hope this doesn't happen again."

Whew, that was a close one. My picture might have been plastered on the walls all over the school. I really hope Jason is right about Ms. Popularity. Someday, I hope he can see the real Brittany that my friends and I have seen.

A couple of hours later, I noticed Brittany talking to the principal while Melody, Melanie, and I were in the cafeteria waiting for the next class to start. I could not hear what she was saying since I was so far away. All I could see was her mouth moving, but I couldn't read her lips.

"I wonder what Brittany is up to now?" I asked.

"I don't know," said Melody. "Who cares? As long as it doesn't involve us in any way, I'm okay."

"I am sorry about what happened earlier," I told Melody.

"No, you don't need to be sorry," said Melody. "It wasn't your fault; it was hers. I had to stand up to her; if I didn't, she would make us miserable forever."

We all glanced up from eating, and Brittany was still talking to the principal. Principal James and Brittany turned their heads and looked our way. When Brittany faced our direction, I noticed she had a black eye. How in the world did she get a black eye? She stretched out her right arm and pointed directly at Melody.

The principal and Brittany came over to our table. Brittany was dressed in her cheerleading outfit, and her hair was in a ponytail, but her eye looked disgusting. It was all black and blue and a little swollen. Principal James was dressed in a black suit, and he had his clipboard in his hand.

"Did you give this nice young lady a black eye?" Principal James asked.

"No, sir," said Melody. "I didn't give her a black eye."

Principal James turned his head toward Brittany, and then he looked back at Melody. "She said you did."

I could not believe it. Brittany has the principal in her favor. Could this get any worse? And indeed, it did get worse, just like I thought it would.

"Come on, young lady," said Principal James. "You're coming with me to my office."

"No! I didn't do it," screamed Melody as she looked back at us. "You have to believe me. I didn't do it. Please! Don't do this to me. I am innocent. I swear I am. Somebody, please help me."

I felt so bad for Melody. I did not know what to do. I knew she didn't do it because Melody was with Melanie and me the whole entire time. Brittany, Melody, and Principal James walked back to the office. Halfway to the office, Brittany turned around and smiled at me. I can't believe her smiling at me; she is so awful. I had a feeling that Brittany framed Melody, and her smiling at me confirmed my intuition. I have to get Melody out of trouble. She doesn't deserve this; no one does.

CHAPTER SIXTEEN

"How could this happen?" I asked Melanie and Stanley as we watched outside the office window.

"She is getting into trouble for something she didn't do," said Melanie.

"This feels like an episode of a crime television show that we watch on Friday nights," said Stanley. "Except it is happening to our friend Melody in real life, and it is not a stage production."

"Stanley, be quiet," I whispered. "We don't want the principal to hear us."

"Okay . . . I am sorry," Stanley said softly. "I will be quiet."

"We have to do something," I said as we watched Melody's tears flow down her face.

"But, what could we do?" Melanie asked. "I mean, she is in serious trouble for a crime she did not commit, and plus, she is trapped and has no way out."

"We all are beginning to sound like those actors on that show," I said with a laugh.

"This is no laughing matter," said Stanley. "I wish I could have seen what happened so that I could help Melody better. I got to lunch as soon as I saw Melody walking with Principal James. Do you think the principal wants to talk to you two?"

"I hope the principal does not want to talk to us," I said.

"I am sure he will since all of us girls were at the scene of the crime," said Melanie.

"But what if the principal does not believe us?" I said as I looked at both Stanley and Melanie. "I mean, he did not believe Melody, and she was telling the truth. Why should he believe us?"

"Because we are well behaved, that's why," said Melanie.

"I know, but that's not a good reason for him to listen to us," I replied.

"Actually, Cynthia," said Stanley, "Melanie is on the right track. Older men do listen to good girls because they always tell the truth. So . . . this might work."

"Well, we could try it," I said. "What could we lose by doing so?"

Meanwhile, in the principal's office, Principal James was confronting Melody about the situation at hand.

"I will ask you for the eighth time," said Principal James. "Why did you punch Brittany in the eye?"

With tears flowing down her eyes like a water fountain, she shouted, "I am honestly telling the truth. I did not do it, even though she did deserve it for being mean to my friend."

"So, you are admitting you did do it, then," said Principal James.

Melody dried her tears with a tissue that was placed in front of her. Melody glanced through the window near the office door and saw Melanie, Stanley, and I look at her.

"No, I am not confessing to a thing," said Melody as she leaned back in her chair and folded her arms. "You can do what you want to me. Because I know the truth, and you are just believing a lie from a girl who makes girls like me miserable."

"Oh, really?" Principal James said sarcastically. "That doesn't sound like the sweet, young Brittany I know." Then he pointed at Melody and said, "You, stay here. Don't go anywhere. I still have to decide your punishment. I have to go to my supplies office in the back. I am out of detention slips."

As Principal James walked back to his supply office, Melanie, Stanley, and I walked in.

"Shush," said Melody as she placed her index finger in front of her mouth. "You don't want him to hear you sneaking in here."

"Are you okay?" I asked Melody.

"Yes. I am fine, now that you guys are with me," said Melody. "He does not believe a thing I say. I don't know what I am going—"

Stanley interrupts Melody to suggest an idea . . . an idea that might work in Melody's favor. "Actually, we are working on this right now. We could tell from behind the window that he did not believe you. So . . . here is what we are going to do. Your sister had this idea that we ask our two cute ladies present here to talk to Principal James. Since these two ladies here are shy and good girls, they might be able to make him believe that you are telling the truth, even though we know that you are. Does that make sense, Melody?"

"So . . . you are saying that either my sister or Cynthia will talk to Principal James," said Melody. "And one of them will try to convince him that I am telling the truth."

"Yes, you got it," said Stanley.

"Well . . . good luck with that," said Melody. "I just hope it works. I am having enough trouble getting him to believe me. I hope he believes one of you."

Then, we heard the sound of big footsteps clomping down the hall. The noise of this person's feet got louder and louder as they approached the office meeting room.

"Hurry, guys," Melody said silently as she looked down the hall. "Someone is coming."

We all ran out quickly and hid underneath the window outside of the office.

At that precise moment, Jason walked by and noticed us squatting by the principal's office window. "What are you guys doing here?" Jason asked. He looked in the window, and a confused expression appeared on his face. "Why is Melody in the principal's office?"

"Shush," I said as Melanie, Stanley, and I pulled him down. "You are going to ruin everything." Once Jason was at our level, I started to explain everything. "I am going to make this short and sweet. Melody got into trouble because Brittany told Principal James that Melody gave her a black eye."

"Ugh . . . I told her to leave you guys alone," said Jason. "She did not listen to me again. Some boyfriend I am—can't even get my girlfriend to listen to me."

"I thought you guys were not dating."

"We're not, but we pretend like we are," said Jason. "It's Brittany's weird little plan that she started when we first met."

"Will you two love birds stop flirting?" Stanley said. "We have to get our friend out of trouble."

Jason and I both said, "We are not flirting," at the same time as we smiled and looked at each other.

"Now, let's play rock, paper, scissors to find out which of you two girls will go in," said Stanley. "We are playing the game a little differently this time—the one that loses goes inside."

I played the paper while Melanie played the scissors.

Stanley confirmed his point. "All right, Cynthia. You lost, so you go in."

I wanted to talk to the principal, anyway. I knew somehow I could change his mind.

As I walked to the door, Jason started teasing me, "Be careful, my lovebird. We will meet again someday soon."

I can't believe he said that. I smiled, thinking of the cute words he just said to me, and I began to giggle. I am glad he made me smile, so I would feel better about convincing Principal James.

I walked in while Melody and Principal James were sitting at the round table in the middle of the room.

"Now, Melody," said Principal James. "I am going to ask you . . ." Principal James heard the door squeak, and he turned his head around. I got his attention quickly. All I had to do was open the door. That didn't take long. Now is my chance to save Melody from injustice.

"Excuse me, Principal James," I said. "Can I talk to you for a moment?"

"Sure, Cynthia, we can talk," said Principal James. "But first, we should move to the back room."

We walked to his smaller office, and I noticed that his desk was centered equally to the back wall. A big, black chair sat alone on the side wall. And a ton of cardboard boxes filled with paper scattered around the sides of the room, which made the area look more like a storage place than an office.

"What would you like to talk about?" Principal James asked me.

"Um, it's about my friend, sir, Melody," I told him. "She has gotten into trouble for something she did not do. I am more of a witness, per se. I was there when this situation occurred."

"You mean that girl out there is your friend?" he asked as he pointed in Melody's direction.

"Yes, she is, sir," I told him. "We have been friends forever."

Principal James started pacing back and forth while he was processing all of this information. I could tell that he was determined to find out the truth, but he seemed to be indecisive on which student to believe. Would he believe Brittany? Melody? Or me? Then, he moved his arm and said, "Go on with your story."

"I want to tell you the truth," I said. "Melody did not hit Brittany in the eye. I saw the whole thing. Brittany was picking on us, and Melody was the one protecting us. I don't know who gave Brittany a black eye, but Melody didn't do it. Please believe me."

In the front office, Melody, Melanie, and Stanley were waiting for us to return.

"What is going on back there?" Melanie asked.

"Maybe this was a bad idea, Stanley," said Melody. "I don't want Cynthia to get into trouble for my wrongdoing."

"But, you didn't do anything wrong," said Stanley.

"Well, I could have if Melanie and Cynthia weren't there to stop me," said Melody. "I rather confess that I did it than to get my best friend in trouble."

Melody was about to get up and confess to Principal James until she saw us coming out of the back room.

"Where did you guys come from?" Principal James asked as he glanced at Melanie and Stanley with a confused expression on his face. Then, he shook his head. "Well, never mind. Ms. Melody, you are free to go. You should thank Cynthia here for telling me everything."

"We did it!" we all shouted while jumping up and down.

As we were leaving the principal's office, we heard the principal getting on the intercom. "Brittany Woods. Come to the office, pronto."

CHAPTER SEVENTEEN

While eating our breakfast at school, we all gathered at our usual table thinking about what happened yesterday.

"Do you think we are going to get into more trouble since we told on Brittany?" Melanie asked as she took a bite of her apple.

"Really, Melanie?" I said. "Do we really have to talk about this?"

"Talk about what?" Jason asked as he sat down beside us.

"Oh, the crazy situation yesterday with Principal James."

"Oh, yeah, that." Jason took a bite out of his sausage biscuit. "How did that go?"

"Actually, it turned out rather well," I told him. "Melody didn't get into trouble, and she is free from whatever punishment the principal was going to give her."

"I am glad that everything turned out okay," said Jason.

"But, we only have one problem," said Melanie.

"Okay . . . what's that?" Jason asked.

"Is Brittany going to make our lives miserable because we told on her?" Melanie asked as she glanced over at her sister Melody, then back at Jason.

Jason glanced over at Melody, then to me, and back at Melanie. Jason appeared to be a little hesitant on how to answer Melanie's question. Jason bit his lip and said confidently, "Don't worry about Brittany. She won't be bothering you guys anymore."

"I hope you are right, Jason," said Melody. "I don't think I can tolerate any more of this."

Melody appeared to be very upset about this whole Brittany

situation. I wish I could tell her something that would make her feel better, but I didn't know what that was. I have never seen her this uptight before. She will snap out of it; I know she will.

In the corner of my eye, I could see Brittany approaching us. I looked at Jason in the eye, and then I tilted my head and moved my eyes to the side to show him that Brittany was coming.

"Jason, I think you are going to have to rephrase your statement. Here she comes, now."

Brittany came over, walking with her hair blowing like she was in a photoshoot. The hallway lights lit up her face so bright that I noticed her black eye was gone. What's up with that? She had a black eye yesterday, and it is gone today. I am so confused. This doesn't make any sense to me. I wanted to ask her, but I didn't have the guts.

An idea about makeup popped into my head. Makeup covers things up really well. So, maybe that's what she used to cover her black eye. I looked at my friends to see if they noticed Brittany's eye, but no one said anything. They all appeared to be as shocked as I was. As she came closer to us, the glamorous side of her faded when she got right in Jason's face.

"Hey, sweetheart. What are you doing with these weirdos?" Brittany asked as she curled up her nose at us. "Jason, you haven't turned into a weirdo, have you? I mean, I thought you were popular. Popular people shouldn't hang out with weirdos. You should be hanging out with me. We are a team, and plus, we are the cutest couple ever." Brittany bent down to Jason's level, and she took a picture with him. "Come back to me, my sweet Jason. You will be better off with me than with them."

I couldn't believe what I was hearing. Everything she said sounded so dramatic and even a little staged, if you know what I mean. It was making me so sick that I wanted to gag. I turned to look at Jason, and he looked at me. He looked so much sadder now than he did before. I felt so sorry for Jason. He can't seem to be himself or hang out with his friends when Brittany is around. While wondering what was going to happen next, I looked up at Brittany in disgust.

"Well? Hello, Jason?" Brittany said annoyingly. "Are you even there? I am talking to you."

"Oh, I am sorry," said Jason. "I was just thinking."

"Why do you need to think?" Brittany was clueless. "It's not that hard of a decision to make."

"Okay, sweetheart," said Jason. "I am coming with you."

"Good," said Brittany. "You just made the best decision of your life."

Jason looked at me with his sad, puppy-dog eyes and left without saying a word.

"No, Jason!" I yelled. I guess he didn't hear me. I turned, facing my friends, and said, "This disgusts me. I can't believe he took her back after all she has done to us."

"Well . . . Cynthia," said Melody, "I guess you are just going to have to accept that Jason is never going to leave Brittany because of his fear of losing his popularity and football."

"Well, to me, he looked like he didn't want to go with Brittany."

"I noticed that, too," said Melanie. "And did anyone else notice that Brittany's black eye disappeared . . . or was I the only one?"

"Yes, I noticed that too," Melody said in an annoyed voice. "I'd like to know how it vanished. After all, I got into trouble for it. Believe me. I don't want to go through that mess again." Melody looked directly at me. "If he didn't want to go with Brittany, he would have stayed here with us, right?"

"Yes, I think so," I said in doubt. "I think Brittany used makeup on her eye to make it appear as if someone gave her a black eye. That's the only possible solution I can think of on how her black eye is now gone. And plus, makeup washes off. There is no way that a real black eye would be gone the next day. That's just impossible."

Melanie points her index finger up in the air as she finished reading a sentence in her book. "That could be a possibility. I have seen many celebrities do it in movies."

"Oh, Melanie," said Melody. "Can we please stop talking about Brittany's black eye? I am getting a headache." Melody bent her elbow with her arm facing upward. She leaned her head to the side and rested her head on the palm of her hand.

"I just don't get it," I said. "I thought Jason was changing. He was acting like he was getting comfortable with being himself, but now, he is back to being his popular self."

"Yes, he was comfortable being himself with us . . . till Brittany showed up," said Melody with a little attitude.

"I miss the real Jason that I had a crush on. I hope the real Jason comes back, so I can see him again." I sighed.

Once school let out, I hurried home as fast as I could. I didn't say bye to any of my friends. I just couldn't talk because of the tears falling down my face. I just wanted to be alone. I didn't want anyone to give me pity, you know? Pity just makes everything worse, if you know what I mean. I finally arrived at my house, and I ran upstairs, hoping no one would see me, but someone did.

I paused on the stairs. "Honey, are you all right?" my mom asked. "You look like you had a difficult day. Do you want to talk about it? When I am having a rough day, talking about it makes me feel better."

"I know you want to help, Mom, but I really don't want to talk about this right now."

"Come on," said my mom. "Let's talk about it. Doing so will make you feel better. I promise."

"Okay, I guess," I said as I shrugged my shoulders. "We can talk about it if you really want to."

We both walked upstairs and went into my room. I sat on my bed while my mom sat at the foot of my bed.

"Okay, before you say anything," said my mom, "is this problem about a boy?"

I perked up from crying. "Yes, it is. How did you know it was about a boy?"

"Well, it's just motherly instincts," said my mom. "You can tell me all about it, sweetheart. I will listen."

"Mom, I am upset. I was just getting to know the real Jason." I suddenly became really nervous, and I unintentionally started to talk really fast. "He has been untrue to himself because everyone likes him as his popular self. I thought we had a real connection. Then his fake girlfriend Brittany takes him away from me."

"Hold on, honey," said my mom. "You are talking way too fast. Can you please repeat what you said? I could not hear you clearly."

"Brittany, his fake girlfriend, took him away from me. I probably will never see him again." I cried some more even though I didn't want to, but I couldn't help it.

My mom gave me a hug and grabbed a tissue to dry my cheeks.

"Let me see if I understand this," said my mom, who is trying to figure this all out. "So, Brittany and Jason are a fake couple. Jason has been showing his real self around you. Brittany couldn't stand how close you two were getting, so she took him back."

I couldn't have said this better myself, I thought as I nodded to my mom.

"Wow, honey. Your life is beginning to sound almost like a soap opera," said my mom. "Sweetheart, don't worry about it. I am sure everything will turn out better in the end."

"Are you 100 percent sure about it?" I asked as I dried my tears.

"Yes, I am very sure that things are going to get better," said my mom as she got up from the bed and walked toward the door. "You just need some time, and it will happen."

The next morning, I got to school early and sat by the fountain. I looked at the angel on top and thought about how pretty she was.

I dragged my hand through the water, which was still cold from the night before. Melody and Melanie approached me from behind and startled me a little bit.

"Are you okay?" Melanie asked.

"You ran home crying without saying goodbye," said Melody.

"You always say bye to us," said Melanie.

"How could you not say bye to us?" Melody asked. "We are your best friends."

"I am sorry, guys," I said as I swirled my hand in the water. "I just had a lot on my mind, that's all."

"You mean . . . about you-know-who?" Melanie asked.

I nodded at Melanie and Melody without looking at them, and I just kept staring at the water.

"I can't believe he did that to you again," said Melody.

At that moment, Melody and Melanie noticed that Jason was walking toward the fountain.

Melody nudged me on the elbow, and I looked away from the fountain noticing a shadow on the ground that was coming toward me. "I think you two need to talk. We will leave you guys alone."

I turned around and looked up at Jason. "How could you do this to me?"

"What did I do?" Jason asked as if he had done nothing wrong. "Why are you so upset with me?"

"You went back to Brittany," I shouted at him as a few tears started flowing down my face. "How could you? I thought you liked me."

Jason and I moved our eyes around the school front yard. A ton of students stared at us. It was very intimidating, even for me. Jason seemed to be intimidated as well.

"I do like you, Cynthia," said Jason quietly as he looked at a crowd of students, then back to me. "Please don't cry. This is all part of my plan that I told you about earlier. I told you I had a plan to get Brittany. I have it all figured out. You just have to wait and see what happens."

By what Jason was telling me, it sounded very interesting. I can't wait to see Jason's plans unfold. From what I have heard, his junior year is going to be an excellent year for him.

CHAPTER EIGHTEEN

My mind has been racing ever since the last time I spoke to Jason. I have been really curious about his plans this year since Jason is a junior and all. I am really going to miss him when he graduates in a year; he has been a really good friend to me. I haven't seen or spoken to him since he found me sitting by the water fountain. The one person I am not going to miss is Brittany; she has made our lives miserable.

I just knew that this year was going to be my best year in high school ever. I was so excited about it that I woke up an hour earlier this morning. Normally, I don't want to get up, but this year just felt different. I got dressed, put on my favorite pink pumps that I always like to wear, and sat on my chair in front of my vanity table. As soon as I picked up my brush to brush my hair, I heard an unfamiliar noise coming from the outside. I sat there for a few moments, trying to figure out what I was hearing. The noise stopped, so I just shrugged my shoulders and continued to brush my hair. A few minutes later, I heard the noise again, and then it continued a couple more times. I got out of my chair and walked toward my window. I pulled back my curtains and looked out the window. I noticed a young guy dressed in a black leather outfit sitting on a motorcycle. To see him even closer, I ran downstairs and opened the window.

I yelled, "Nice bike you have there."

The young man looked up and started looking around. He couldn't seem to find the person who was talking to him.

I giggled and repeated my sentence again. "Nice bike you have there."

He looked right at me and said, "Thank you."

I didn't recognize who he was since he still had his helmet on. I walked outside and sat on the steps. I placed my hands on the sides of my face, and I just sat there watching him. The young man got off his bike, and he began to walk toward me. A sudden fear of nervousness rushed through my body. I didn't know this person, and he was coming right to me. Maybe he thinks I am someone else. He appeared to be cute, but it was still hard to tell who he was. The young man started to take off his helmet. He unhooked the strap and placed his helmet under his left arm. I wasn't looking directly at him, but I could still see what he was doing by the shadows on the concrete.

"Why aren't you looking at me?" the young man asked. "I hope I didn't frighten you."

Still, without looking at him, I said, "Actually, I am not frightened. I am just really nervous."

"Don't be nervous," he said. "Do you want to take a ride with me to school?"

I was thinking, *well, I don't know you that well.*

The young man held out his hand, and I looked up at him. I could not believe who it was. The motorcyclist was Jason. Since when did he get a motorcycle? He looked so different that I didn't even recognize him. I have been crushing on him forever, and I just didn't put the two together. I can't believe how much he has changed in just a few weeks.

"Why didn't you tell me it was you, Jason?" I asked. "I didn't recognize you. You look so different."

"Oh! I thought you knew who I was, sorry about that," said Jason. "No wonder you wouldn't look at me." We both laughed. "I wanted to change my look, so I just trimmed my hair a bit and bought this really cool biker suit."

I was missing his longer hair, but I liked his new look.

"Cynthia, I don't know how to say this, but I am going to try the best I can. I really enjoy the time we have together," said Jason as he sat down next to me on the steps. "I can be myself with you, and I like that. Other people expect me to be the popular football player, but when I am with you, I don't have to be that other guy."

I looked directly at Jason and said, "I like it when you are this guy. I hope I don't see that other guy around that doesn't know I exist." I laughed some more. "You're that other guy, especially around your team and Brittany."

"I know. I do that," said Jason. "I'm very sorry. I just get nervous, and all choked up. I forget that I am hurting the people that I love the most when I turn into the other guy."

Did I hear Jason say the L-word? At that moment, I quietly giggled and smiled with a romantic expression on my face.

Jason didn't recognize that he said the love word and continued on talking. "If I turn into the other guy, don't take what I say seriously. I am just trying to be cool in front of the guys and girls."

"But, you don't have to be that guy," I said. "If your friends don't like you for who you are, then they are not really your true friends. True friends will stick by you, no matter what."

Jason looked up at me and said, "I really hope you are right, Cynthia. I have been the other guy for so long that I don't know how to be me."

"You are being you at this very moment," I told him. "When you are talking to your other friends, just pretend you are talking to me, and you will be fine."

"Okay, I will work on it," said Jason. Jason stood up and grabbed my hand. "Come on. Let's go for a ride; it will be a lot of fun."

"I have never ridden on a motorcycle before," I said as I put on my sunglasses.

"Oh, you will be fine," said Jason. "All you have to do is wear your helmet and hold on to me."

I got up and walked next to him as we walked to his bike. He handed me a helmet, and I placed it on my head. He placed on his helmet; then he sat on his bike.

I sat behind him, and he turned his head around to look at me. "Are you ready to go?"

"Yes, I am ready," I replied with a smile.

He started his engine, and we drove down the street. The cool breeze brushed gently against my face as we rode toward the sunset. The sun looked so beautiful as it set in the sky. I was having the time of my life. It felt as if I were in a dream, but it was all too real. I couldn't imagine how this moment could get any more romantic.

As Jason and I were riding down the street, I glanced up and looked at the sun. I couldn't believe how beautiful the sun looked with its rays beaming a bright pink and orange color. To me, the color kind of reminded me of a sorbet popsicle. Thinking of a popsicle was starting to make me hungry.

"Cynthia, doesn't this weather feel so beautiful today?" said Jason. "I wish we would have more days like this."

While still thinking about the popsicle, I said, "What did you say?" I couldn't believe I didn't hear what my crush was saying to me. I always listen to everything he says, but I guess I was so nervous about being with him that I just couldn't focus, and plus, I was hungry too from skipping breakfast this morning. I always get a little light-headed when I am hungry, so that makes me even more nervous.

We had a couple of minutes of silence then Jason continued to speak. "The weather is so beautiful."

"Oh, yes," I replied. "The weather is very nice, Jason."

"Cynthia, are you okay?" Jason asked. "You seem a little distracted this morning."

"Yes, I am fine," I said. "Well, I am a little hungry."

"Oh, great!" said Jason. "You just read my mind. I want to take you to this little diner up the street. They serve breakfast all day long, and they have the best desserts in town. My favorite is their key lime pie."

"Oh, that sounds delicious," I said. "I can't wait to try their food. I always pass this place on my way to school, but I have never been inside."

Jason and I turned past a sign that read, "Blue Starz Diner: Eat everything delicious at one-stop, $5.99 for breakfast and lunch specials, and free coffee." The restaurant was appealing on the outside with its small parking lot and blue and silver paneling on the building. The diner reminds me of the diners I noticed in my grandma's magazines that I used to read when I was little. The diner wasn't really busy from the few cars I saw in the parking lot, but I thought the diner was pretty, and by the sign, the food seemed inexpensive. Jason and I got off the motorcycle, and we walked across the parking lot.

I couldn't help but notice how cute Jason looked in his black leather outfit as he walked in front of me to the entrance of the diner. His posture was straight, and he seemed more confident now than he did on the day of the Beyond the Sea dance. However, I was still as nervous as I was on the ride over here. I don't know why I am so nervous. I guess I am nervous about being with Jason. But . . . I have been out with him before. Maybe because last time I was at the Blue Freeze ice cream shop and the hospital. Those didn't feel much like dates per se since I asked him to join me at the ice cream shop. But this one seemed more like a formal date than the others, even though I pretended like the other occasions were dates too. Oh, and then I started to think about Brittany. What if she was inside? Oh gosh, that would be the worst possible thing that could happen to Jason and me.

The inside of the diner was equally appealing as the outside. It was beautiful . . . with its light blue walls, alternating white and blue floor tiles, and white and dark blue seats. We stood there for a few moments until a guy about our age approached us.

"Welcome to Blue Starz Diner. How many will be dining with us today?"

Jason pointed two fingers at the host, and the guy walked us to our table. As we were walking, the host started to talk to us; he seemed really friendly.

"Have you guys been here before?" the guy asked.

"Yes, I have," said Jason. "But my friend here hasn't."

I looked at the guy's name tag, which read Zachary. Zach seemed very interested in us as he continued on asking Jason and me questions.

"Who is this beautiful girl?" Zachary asked. "Is she your sister?"

I couldn't believe this guy. He seemed more interested in me than Jason was at the moment. I laughed and rolled my eyes at how silly this guy was being. He is a total flirt. "No, we are just friends." He was cute, by the way, but I was still more interested in Jason.

"You guys seem very familiar, but I can't place your faces. Maybe it will come to me." Zach placed down our menus on our table and said, "Well, you two enjoy your meal."

While Jason and I were looking at our menus, Zachary went over to the drink counter. Standing behind the drink counter was a girl with long, dark hair that was a little below shoulder length. She was wearing a white shirt, dark pants, and an apron. She was fixing tea when she noticed Zachary approaching her. She looked up at him while she was pouring tea into two glass cups.

"What do you want, Zachary?" she said. "I am a little busy right now. I am not in the mood for your flirtatious shenanigans. I know you think I am hot, which I am, but can you go flirt with someone else?"

"Wait . . . no," said Zachary as he shook his head. "I don't want to flirt with you, Veronica."

"You don't?" Veronica asked. "Are you sick?"

"Really?" said Zachary. "You had to bring that one up?"

"Yes," said Veronica. "I was just asking to make sure because you always want to flirt with me or some other girl in here."

Zachary makes a funny face and looks straight ahead, and points to the table where Jason and Cynthia are sitting. "Do you know those two? They look so familiar to me."

"You probably have seen them here before," said Veronica without looking at the table. "It's a small town, remember? Besides, you probably have seen them at school."

Then Zachary yells softly, "Yes! That's exactly where I have seen them . . . at school."

Veronica placed her two filled tea glasses on a tray and looked at where Zachary was pointing. "Oh my gosh!" she yelled as she dropped her iced tea tray, which caused the glass to shatter all over the floor. "I know exactly who they are; that's Jason and Cynthia. I can't believe that they would show their faces in here, after what we did to them."

"What did we do to them?" Zachary asked unknowingly.

"Ugh, Zach, you don't remember?" Veronica asked as she started to pick up the broken pieces of glass while wearing gloves. Veronica pointed in the direction of Jason and Cynthia while sitting in the frog position on the floor. "Remember when Brittany hired us to take pictures of her boyfriend at the dance?"

"Yes, I do," said Zachary.

Veronica stood up, "Well, that's them."

"Oh, yeah. I remember now. I was working in the security camera room, and I watched it until I saw Cynthia and Jason together. I took a ton of pictures of them that night. Then you plastered them all over the hallway, with Brittany's help, by the way."

"Exactly," said Veronica.

"Well, this is going to be very awkward for you," said Zachary in a slight chuckle. "They are in your section. You are going to have to wait on them."

"Ugh, Zach," said Veronica as she placed two new tea glasses on a tray and walked away, saying, "you are so annoying."

Back at Cynthia and Jason's table, Jason and Cynthia are still browsing their menus while unaware of their surroundings. Jason looked up from his menu and looked around the diner. He glanced at his watch and looked at Cynthia.

"I don't know why it is taking so long," said Jason. "They usually take our order by now."

"I guess they are extra busy this morning," I added.

"Oh, wait . . . here comes someone now," said Jason.

"Hi, I am sorry about the wait. I had to clean up a mess in the back." She took out a pen that she had behind her ear and said, "My name is Veronica. May I take your order?"

"Hi, Veronica," said Jason. "I will have coffee and a waffle with eggs and toast."

"What will you have?" Veronica asked as she looked at me.

I looked up at her. I could sense that she was a little nervous, but to me, she seemed to be hiding her nervousness very well. "Um, I will have a cheese omelet, bacon, and a sweet tea." I felt very grown-up ordering tea. I usually drink milk or juice for breakfast.

Then Jason started to speak, "Um . . . Veronica, you look so familiar. Where have I seen you before?"

"Umm." She fluffed her hair to the side and started giggling flirtatiously with Jason. She smiled. "Maybe you have seen me here. You do come in here a lot."

"No, I don't think that's it," said Jason. "I think I have seen you somewhere else. I just can't put my finger on it."

I was kind of getting annoyed that Jason was so interested in this girl. In my opinion, I didn't think Veronica was his type, but then again, as I looked at her, maybe she was. She had a nice complexion, beautiful hair, a pretty smile, and a nice figure that looked physically fit like a cheerleader. I looked at her, smiling at Jason while twirling her hair. She was like the total package. She had that look that a lot of guys in my school want. I was starting to get depressed at the thought of losing Jason to Veronica. Then it just hit me—Veronica might be one of Brittany's squad members. How could I have not seen this before? I had all the clues right in front of me, but I just didn't put them together until now. I wanted to tell Jason what I figured out, but I couldn't with her standing there. So, I just continued listening to their conversation.

"Well, maybe, Jason," said Veronica, "I just have one of those faces."

"Hey," said Jason in a shocked voice. "How did you know my name?"

"What? Did I say Jason?" Veronica said. "I didn't mean to say your name. I will be right back with your drinks."

"How?" Jason said with a puzzled look on his face. "How did she know my name? I don't even know her."

Now was a good time as any to tell Jason what I had just figured out. "Jason, I just figured out where you have seen Veronica . . . she goes to our school."

"She does?" Jason said while still in his puzzled look. "How do you know this?"

"I remember her in Brittany's posse when she was talking to Melody, Melanie, and me when Brittany took my envelope from me. I also saw her when Brittany wanted Stanley to sit at the popular table with them.”

Jason’s face went from being confused to shocked. “Brittany wanted Stanley to sit at the popular table. That’s unusual.” Then his face went from shocked to sad. “Oh, wow, I can’t believe I didn’t see this before. I mean, of all people, I should have recognized Veronica as a cheerleader. I am on the football team.”

“Well. It’s okay, Jason,” I said. “You know who she is now.”

“You know what?” Jason asked. “She seemed to be very nervous. Do you know why?”

Well, I would be nervous too if I were waiting on a hot guy that looked like Jason, but I couldn’t say that to him. Sometimes I think Jason is unaware of how attractive he is to other girls, but at other times, I think he is aware of his good looks. Since I have been talking to him, he doesn’t seem concerned about his appearance. And why would he be? He is so cute. I smiled nervously at him and said, “I have no idea why she was so nervous.”

Veronica came back and placed our drinks on our table. “Here’s one coffee for you, and here is your sweet tea.” After that, she looked at Jason. “Do you want any sugar for your coffee, Jason?”

“Yes, please,” said Jason.

“Your meals will be coming up in just a few minutes,” said Veronica as she walked toward the back of the diner.

“I can’t believe you keep calling him Jason,” said Zachary. “We aren’t supposed to act like we know them. They are going to get suspicious of us.”

“No, they are not,” said Veronica. “They have no idea that we were involved in Brittany's little scheme. And besides, they are never going to find out our little secret. So, let's keep it that way."

"I know this is going to sound crazy," said Zachary. "But since they have been here, that whole situation is coming back to memory, and it is starting to make me feel guilty for what I have done. They seem so nice to me. I think one of us should tell them the truth."

"No, you wouldn't dare!" Veronica shouted as she picked up Jason's and Cynthia's plates. "If you do tell them, which I hope you won't . . . don't do it here."

"Here comes our food," I said to Jason as I noticed Veronica carrying a tray over to our table.

"It's about time," said Jason. "I'm starving."

To me, Veronica seemed a little stressed and tired. She carried the tray over and placed each of our plates in front of us on the table. Veronica smiled at each of us and said, "Enjoy your meal." And then she left to visit another customer.

"This looks so delicious, Jason," I said as I looked down at my omelet and bacon arranged nicely on the plate in front of me. "Thank you so much for bringing me here." I laid my arm across the table, hoping that he would want to hold my hand.

Jason glanced up from eating and noticed that my arm was across the table, and he held out his hand to hold mine. "You're welcome. I am having a great time with you."

Not long after that, our breakfast date was over, and we exited the diner. I was sad to see that our date was almost over, but I was happy that I got to spend time with Jason. I couldn't believe that I actually got to hold his hand. The touch of his hand and how it felt will be something I will never forget. How romantic! If Jason and I were in an animated cartoon, I could almost picture little red hearts floating above my head. Oh, and the conversation we had was nice too. I was hoping this date would last forever, but I knew it wouldn't since we both have to be at school. As we walked to Jason's motorcycle, we heard footsteps coming our way.

"Wait up, guys! Wait up!" a guy hollered behind us. "Wait up!"

Jason and I both turned around, and we noticed it was Zachary. This reminded me of the time when Jason was hollering for me at the hospital.

Zachary was out of breath and tired. "I have something . . . uh . . . I have to . . . tell . . . you. It has been bothering me since you both came to the diner."

"What?" Jason and I said together.

"What is bothering you?" I asked. He seemed like such a nice guy.

Zachary spoke again, and he seemed to be very upset. "I did it. I am so sorry."

Jason and I looked at each other in confusion. I looked at Zachary as I noticed his sweat dripping down his face. I felt sorry for him. He was trying to tell Jason and me something, but for some reason, he couldn't get his confession out. Was he afraid of our reaction? Or maybe he had done something awful, and he was having trouble admitting it. What could Zachary have done that would have made him this upset?

"Did what?" Jason asked as his face went from a smile to serious.

"I was working the security camera the night of the dance. I took photos of you both while you were kissing. I know now that I shouldn't have done it. It didn't bother me when I did it, but now since I have met you both, I feel just plain awful."

"Why you?" Jason shouted as he clenched his hand and started to move it toward Zachary's face. Zachary saw the punch coming, and he slowly moved his head back.

I didn't like what was happening. I don't think violence is the answer to this situation. As Jason got his fist closer to Zachary's face, I yelled, "No! Jason. Violence is not the answer."

Jason looked down at his clenched hand and realized what he was about to do. He unclenched his hand and moved his arm to his side. "I know," said Jason. "I am sorry, dude. But . . . that whole situation ruined our lives. I can't believe you were a part of it."

"I am so sorry, Jason," said Zachary. "I wish I could take back what I did, but . . . I can't. If I could go back in time, I would change what I did. Honestly . . . I would."

Jason pointed at me and gave Zachary a disappointed look. "You hurt this pretty girl too."

"I know," said Zachary as he looked at me with the saddest expression on his face. "I am so sorry, cutie."

Wow! I had two guys calling me attractive. But . . . why did it have to be in this awkward situation?

Jason wrapped his arm behind my shoulder and said, "Come on, let's go."

We both got on the motorcycle, and Jason drove off. I looked over my shoulder, and Zachary was still standing there with the saddest look on his face.

I felt so sorry for Zachary on the ride back to school. All I could see was a picture of his sad face in my mind. I couldn't help but wonder if Jason was too hard on him. I understand both sides of the situation. Jason wanted to punch Zachary out for the misery he had caused us. And Zachary feeling guilty for what he had done. But, what I couldn't understand was Zachary's reason for doing it. At least he told us he did it, so we should forgive him, right?

I kept pondering the situation as Jason and I were walking up the curb toward the entrance of the school. Everyone was staring at us again. I guess it was the sight of us two walking together that surprised them. He walked ahead of me while I followed. I rather enjoyed the walk with Jason, but we didn't speak a word to each other. I guess he had too much on his mind as I did. Jason held the door open for me as we both walked in together. He didn't stop to say goodbye or see you later. He just continued on walking straight down the hall until I couldn't see him anymore.

I was crushed until I saw my best friends sitting at our usual table. Melody was eating an apple while she was sitting on the table with her feet placed on the seat. Stanley was trying to finish his homework that he didn't do the night before. Melanie was drawing a tiger for her art class. And I sat down next to Melanie as I watched her draw.

"You know, Stanley?" Melody said. "I don't know why you don't do your homework the night before, instead of rushing through it now."

"Oh, come on, Melody," said Stanley as he placed his pencil on the table. "Give a guy a break. I was busy last night. I am sure you don't finish everything all the time."

I was starting to wonder what Stanley was doing last night. He usually finishes all of his homework before the next morning.

"Yes, I did all of my homework," said Melody as she seemed to be annoyed with Stanley.

There was a slight pause, and then I started to talk. "Stanley, what did you do last night? I am interested in hearing about it."

Stanley was shocked that I was interested. His eyes got big, and he tilted his head to the side. "Really?" said Stanley. "I wasn't really going to bring it up, but . . . I was practicing."

The thought that was going through my mind was, *what is he practicing?* It could be anything. We all had confused expressions on our faces, trying to figure out what Stanley was trying to tell us.

After Stanley saw all of our confused faces, he said, "I think I am going to try out for the baseball team."

We were all shocked; each of us had our jaws dropped. We knew Stanley liked baseball, but we didn't think he would actually try out.

"Don't you think I should?" He asked in a worried voice.

"Oh yes," said Melody. "I think you should try out."

"Me too," said Melanie. "I think that would be fun for you. We were just shocked that you wanted to try out because we didn't think you wanted to be on the high school team since coach Handeler fussed at you for eating in class."

"Yeah, I remember that," said Stanley. "I was really hungry that day, too. If I join, I will not let him bother me."

"Stanley, I think you should try out for the baseball team," I said. "You would be a great player."

"Well, thanks, Cynthia," said Stanley. "I might definitely do it now since we are all in agreement. Anyway, enough about me. Does anyone have any interesting gossip to share?"

Well, here is my moment to share my story about Jason and me. I have wanted to tell them about this since I first sat down. "I do. Jason and I went to a diner to eat breakfast this morning."

"What?" Melody shouted. "I was wondering why Jason walked in with you this morning."

"This is going to be interesting," said Stanley. "Jason is the talk of the school once again."

"I know," I said as I started to giggle.

"Go on," said Melanie. "This is very interesting. I need to know all of the details."

I knew they would be excited to hear this. *It's not every day a girl like me goes out with a popular boy*, I thought, as I started to giggle some more.

"Did he pick you up?" Melanie asked.

"Yes, he did," I squealed. "He picked me up in his motorcycle. I didn't know it was him at first with his new haircut and outfit."

"Oh. My. Gosh. He has a motorcycle," said Melody. "How was the motorcycle ride? I always wanted to ride one."

"It was great . . . and the breeze . . . was amazing," I said in a dreamy way. "I was a little nervous. Jason could tell that I was a little distracted, so he asked me if I was okay. I told him I was fine, but then I spoke up and told him that I was hungry. Jason was excited, and he said he wanted to take me to Blue Starz Diner."

Stanley was quiet till the moment I mentioned Blue Starz Diner.

"Oh, I know that place," said Stanley. "I have been there a couple of times."

Since when did Stanley go there? I have never heard him mention Blue Starz Diner before.

"They have really good food and great prices," Stanley added.

"When have you been?" I asked Stanley.

"I went a lot during the summer while you guys were at Brittany's party. I mean . . . I went after I felt better."

That made sense to me, and I continued my conversation. "After we got inside, we met two very interesting people. Zachary, our host, and Veronica, our waitress. Zachary was really friendly, and he even flirted at me . . . right in front of Jason too."

"What did Jason do?" Melanie asked.

"He didn't do anything but continued talking to Zachary."

"That figures," said Melody. "I thought he would get jealous."

"Nope, he didn't," I said as I shook my head from side to side. "But Jason was really sweet to me. We held hands as we ate."

"Oh, how romantic," said Melanie. "What else happened?"

"Well, Jason and Veronica had a nice chat while I sat there. Veronica even mentioned his name in their conversation a couple of times like she knew who he was. Jason was unclear on who Veronica was, and he wasn't sure how she knew his name. Then, all of a sudden, it hit me. I have seen Veronica in Brittany's posse every time Brittany comes over to pick on us."

"Oh!" said Stanley as he focused his attention on me. "This is starting to get very interesting now."

I knew Stanley would get interested in this part. He likes hearing about all of the drama that cheerleaders go through. I am unaware of why he gets so interested, but he does. I began to laugh at Stanley, and then I continued speaking. "For some strange reason, Veronica and Zachary seemed to be very nervous around Jason and me."

"Why would they be nervous around you and Jason?" Melanie asked.

"I am not sure."

"Did you find out later?" Melody asked in a concerned voice.

"I found out more than I wanted to know about why Zachary was so nervous," I said. "But nothing from Veronica."

"What?" Stanley said in shock. "Did you find out some dark secret about him?"

"Apparently . . . I did," I said. "Jason and I were both upset about it. More so, Jason. He was so upset that he almost punched the guy out."

"Oh. Come on, Cynthia," said Melanie. "Please tell us what happens next."

I like telling them all of these juicy details first to keep them interested. Then, I lay the biggest one down last. It's similar to what a movie or a television show's climax does to us, but I do it just with words, with no videos or pictures. I continued to tell them more until I told the last juiciest detail.

"After we ate, we walked out of the restaurant. Jason and I both heard someone's footsteps running behind us. We both turned around, and it was Zachary. He was very much out of breath, and he gaspingly, one word at a time, apologized to both of us. Jason and I were very confused at that moment. We weren't sure why Zachary was apologizing to us. Zachary started explaining his whereabouts and what he did the night of the dance. He said he was working the security camera that night, and he took pictures of Jason and me while we were kissing in front of the school."

"He did it?" Melody shouted. "I can't believe he would stoop that low. Why on earth would he do that? He doesn't even know you."

"Not sure, but for some reason, I think Brittany put him up to it. I am not sure how Veronica fits into this whole thing. But, I am not sure if I want to find out."

Later that night, I just couldn't focus on my math homework. I just stared and stared at the problem. I must have read this equation one hundred times. I am usually out on a Friday night, but Stanley, Melody, and Melanie were busy. So, I was just stuck at home figuring out this math problem. I might as well get my homework done now than do it this weekend. And plus, if I do my homework now, I will have more free time on Saturday and Sunday to do whatever I want. Now, back to math. We are trying to solve a system of linear equations.

The problem read:

$$5x-2y= 6$$
$$-3x+y= -3$$

Solve for X and Y

To me, these problems are simple, but I was too worried about Jason to concentrate. I haven't seen or heard from him all day since breakfast. I hate to see him hurt like this. He seemed really upset when he walked into school this morning. He just went ahead of me without saying a word and kept on walking down the long, narrow hallway.

While still thinking about Jason, I got off my bed and walked over to my vanity table where my phone was placed. I started to brush my hair, and then I looked over at my phone. I noticed that I had a message from someone. I put my brush down on the table and picked up my cell phone. I opened the message. I was so shocked that I received a message from this person that I had to re-read the message again to make sure I wasn't daydreaming.

> Hey, Cynthia. I had fun at the diner this morning.
> I need to talk to you. Can you meet me at the
> beach around eleven tomorrow morning?
> Your friend, Jason.

CHAPTER NINETEEN

The sun was shining so brightly in the morning sky. The sunlight's rays warmed my face with its touch. The sun felt so good on my face and body. I was lying down on a towel at the beach while waiting for Jason to meet me here at this very spot.

As I laid there waiting, I suddenly became very hot. I was thinking that Jason should hurry up because I was starting to melt, and so was the food. I brought sandwiches, chips, and soda in a pink picnic basket. You know I have to get every accessory in the color pink. Anyway, as I rolled over on my stomach, I decided to look inside the basket to see if the food was okay. As I opened the picnic basket, I felt a light tap on my shoulder. I paused for a moment and slowly turned around.

"Hey, you scared me," I yelled as I started throwing sand on him.

Jason tried to cover himself from getting sand on him, but that didn't work.

"Hey, is this really necessary?" Jason said as he chuckled. "I just bought this shirt yesterday."

"I like your new shirt, Jason," I said with a laugh. "The sand adds an elegant touch to your outfit."

"Oh, thank you," said Jason as he looked at me in the eyes and smiled. "I thought I would go with the sandy look today. I think it suits me quite well. Don't you think?"

"Yes, it does, Jason." I couldn't stop laughing. I would try to stop, but every time I looked at Jason, I would start laughing all over again. What he said was just too funny.

Jason kneeled down on the towel beside me, and he looked at the picnic basket. "Nice colorful basket," said Jason. "In your favorite color, I might add."

I could not believe he still remembers my favorite color.

Jason looked up at me and smiled, and then he looked down at the picnic basket. "What did you bring us to eat, my sweet?"

My cheeks turned red when I heard him call me his sweet. "I brought sandwiches, chips, and sodas."

Jason grabbed a sandwich and unwrapped the aluminum foil. He took a bite out of his ham sandwich. He placed his wrapped sandwich on the towel and reached in the picnic basket for a small bag of barbecue chips. After Jason grabbed some chips, I reached in my basket for the turkey sandwich that I wrapped and sealed with a pink butterfly sticker. I ate a few bites of my sandwich, and then I realized I had forgotten to grab some chips. I placed my wrapped sandwich on my lap, and I reached inside my pink basket for some chips. I couldn't decide which one to choose since I brought with me an assortment of my favorite flavors. So, in just three seconds, I decided to pick the nacho cheese one.

"This sandwich is really good," said Jason as he ate another bite.

"Do you want a soda?"

"Yes, I do," said Jason.

I placed down my sandwich and handed him a drink.

"Thanks, Cynthia," said Jason.

"You're welcome," I said. Knowing that Jason wanted to talk to me made me even more nervous to talk to him. I had no idea what he wanted to ask me. I was kind of freaking out. I just didn't know what words to use, so I did the best I could at that moment. "Umm . . . Jason, you said in the text message you sent me earlier that you wanted to talk to me. What would you like to talk about?"

"We can talk about anything you want to," said Jason.

"Oh . . . I thought you had something specific you wanted to ask me."

Jason became quiet and sad again, like the time I saw him at the water fountain. He began to stare at the sand for a few minutes while pondering what he wanted to say to me. The few minutes of silence were very awkward for me.

"Well, Cynthia . . . I don't know how to put this," said Jason.

Oh, great, I thought. His first sentence doesn't sound promising. My mind began to race, thinking about all of the worst possible things he could say to me at this very moment, ranging from he thinks I am ugly to he doesn't want to see me again. I already know how it felt when I thought he didn't want to see me again, which wasn't even true, by the way. I longed to know what he had to say. I was so shaken up inside. I just wanted to get this part over with, so I could feel better. The tears began to fall down my cheeks, and I was getting more anxious as I waited.

Jason looked up at me and asked, "Cynthia, are you okay?"

"I am fine, Jason. Please continue what you were saying."

"All right," he said as he picked up a napkin and gave it to me. He had this sad expression on his face when he looked at me.

"I hate to see a girl cry," he said. "Is there anything you want to talk about?"

"No, Jason. I want to hear what you have to say."

"Okay," said Jason as he repeated what he said earlier. "Well, Cynthia. I don't know how to put this. But, I am very sorry for what I put you through last year. I have been struggling for a while now, trying to find my true self. Everyone is expecting me to be someone that I am not, and every time I am with you, I am the person I want to be."

"Wow, Jason, you are making me teary-eyed again," I told him. "What you said was just so beautiful. I wish I could say something that beautiful."

"You can if you put your heart in it," said Jason. "It is about time I listened to mine. Ever since the first time I saw you, I thought you were the prettiest girl I have ever seen. I just could not admit it because I was being forced to date Brittany at the time, and also, I was pretending to be someone I am not. I don't know what is going to happen to us in the next couple of days or in the future." Jason looked down at the sand and sighed, and then he looked right back at me. "If you can forgive me for what I have done, I would be really happy if you would come with me to the Junior Ring dance. I haven't asked any other girl. I have saved this one question for you. If you don't want to come with me, then I will understand. I just hope that I don't become the popular guy before the dance. What do you say, Cynthia?" he asked as he held my hand. "Will you go to the Junior Ring dance with me?"

I was super nervous and excited at the same time.

"Yes. Yes!" I told him in a slight scream. "I will go to the dance with you."

"I was so worried that you were going to say no," said Jason. "You just made me the happiest guy in the world."

We were both so excited about going to the dance together that we instantly embraced each other. After we hugged, we both looked into each other's eyes. Jason and I slowly moved our heads closer to each other, our lips finally touched, and we had our second kiss. Our second kiss was so magical. I felt like a princess who had just found her prince and lived happily ever after.

CHAPTER TWENTY

I was so excited about the day I had with Jason that I immediately called Melody and Melanie right when I got home from shopping. I used the phone upstairs so that my family wouldn't hear all of the juicy details. I picked up my pink princess phone and dialed their number.

"Hey guys, I have some exciting news."

"Ooh," said Melody and Melanie together.

"What exciting news do you have to tell us?" Melanie asked.

"This better be good, Cynthia," said Melody. "We did not get to talk yesterday because you were gone all day. Where were you?"

"I am sorry about that," I told them. "I just wanted to tell you that this info will be worth the wait."

It is kind of funny because we are probably the only friends that don't say hi much on the phone. We would much rather start talking.

"You know the guy I talk about all the time?"

"Yes, we know the one," said Melody. "You mean lover boy, Jason."

"Yes, him," I said with a giggle. "Jason sent me a text saying that he wanted to talk to me."

"Did he ask you out?" Melody asked.

"Hold on, Melody," I replied with a chuckle. "I haven't finished the story yet."

"Well . . . hurry up," said Melody. "We are dying to hear the rest."

"So, I agreed to meet Jason at the beach. I packed sandwiches, chips, and some sodas. I was laying on a beach towel waiting for him to show up when all of a sudden, I got a gentle tap on my shoulder."

"Wow, he actually showed up," said Melody. "That's awesome."

"He must really like you, Cynthia," said Melanie.

I glanced in the mirror, and I saw that I was blushing. I am so glad that my friends didn't see this; they would have been teasing me like crazy. I just couldn't quit smiling. I was so excited about the time I had with Jason. I couldn't wait to tell them the rest of my story. "We felt really connected, and he was very open to me about what he was going through."

"Aw, that's really sweet," said Melanie.

"I am not done yet," I giggled. "I have one more thing to say. He grabbed my hand gently, apologized for the past, and he asked me to his Junior Ring dance."

Melody and Melanie screamed in my ear. My friends were screaming so loud that I had to move the phone away from my ear. It felt like they were right next to me. Their scream reminded me of the time when a girl I knew in kindergarten screamed every time she ran while playing Duck, Duck, Goose. When they were done screaming, I placed the phone back by my ear.

"I can't believe he asked me out, either. I mean, I am the girl who never gets asked out by a popular boy."

"We are so happy for you," said Melanie.

The way we were talking, it sounded like Jason and I were about to get married.

"What are you going to wear to the dance?" Melody asked.

"Well . . . I found this dress, which is sparkling pink on top, and the skirt is pink satin."

"I think I know which one you are talking about," said Melanie. "Is it the one that is near the front window of Styling Stars Fashions?"

"Yes," I said. "That's the one I want to buy."

"Wow! That's a beautiful dress, Cynthia," said Melody. "How about all of us, including your mom, go to Styling Stars to buy the dress? It will be fun to go together since the Junior Ring dance is a special occasion, you know?"

"Okay, that sounds like fun," I said. "We will meet you both down there in a few minutes."

I was so excited about buying my beautiful dress that I flew down the stairs so fast that I almost fell.

My mom was in the kitchen doing dishes when she yelled, "What in the world is all that racket?"

"It's me, Mom," I replied. "Mom, I got asked to the Junior Ring dance by Jason, and I found the perfect dress."

"Where did you find this perfect dress?" my mom asked.

"At Styling Stars," I answered. "Melody and Melanie are going to come with us."

"You are going with Jason?" she asked in her surprised voice. "That was sweet of him to ask you. I sure hope that he doesn't hurt you again. You have gone through enough with that boy."

"He said he would not hurt me again."

"I sure hope you are right, honey," said my mom. "If buying this dress and going out with Jason will make you happy, then . . . I am all for buying this dress."

I grabbed my phone out of my pocket and sent a text message to Melody and Melanie:

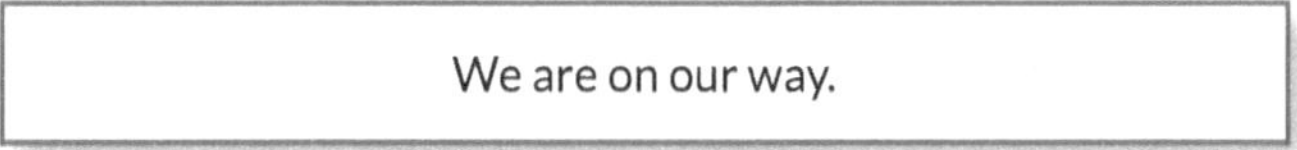

We arrived at the boutique as Melody and Melanie were staring at the pink, sparkly dress in the window display. The dress was so pretty; the light of the sun made it shine even more.

My mom stepped in front of Melody and Melanie. "Is this the one you want to buy?"

"Yes. It is, Mom."

"Oh, honey . . . it's absolutely beautiful," said my mother. "You picked out the prettiest dress in the store. You are going to look so beautiful in that. I hope they have your size."

We walked over to the clothing rack, and I picked up a few different sizes of the same dress. I walked over to the fitting room and tried on each dress. The first dress was way too snug. I couldn't breathe in that one, so I took it off fast. The second one fit quite nicely on me. It was my favorite so far. The third dress was way too big. I put that one back on the hanger in my dressing room. The second one I tried on fit the best, so I put that one on again. I looked in the mirror, fixed my hair, and twirled around a couple of times. When I was ready, I opened the door and walked out of the fitting room, where my mom and best friends were sitting. Everyone was smiling, and they loved my dress. I felt like a beautiful princess just waiting for her prince to arrive. I even saw Melanie and Melody do a high five. Right then and there, I knew this was the right dress for me.

The next day at school, I heard everyone gossiping about Jason. I don't know what he had done, but everyone was talking about it. With everyone talking about him, it made me even more curious to find out what he had done, but I couldn't find anyone who would tell me. I was getting so worried about him. I hope he wasn't sick or hurt. As I walked around some more, I noticed a large crowd of students gathering in the cafeteria listening to someone. I couldn't tell who it was at first with everyone standing in front of them. But as I got closer, I immediately recognized the couple. It was Jason and Brittany. What are they doing together? I wanted to know what all of the commotion was about, so I stood there to listen to what she had to say.

"Hello, fellow students," said Brittany. "I am so glad that all of you are here."

I thought, *since when is Brittany excited to see anybody?*

Brittany fluffed her hair to the side and grabbed ahold of Jason's hand. "Jason and I are going to the ring dance together."

Melanie, Melody, and Stanley all appeared from the crowd and stood next to me with disgusted looks on their faces.

"If you would be so kind as to vote for us instead of Katharine and James, I will make sure you won't regret your decision," said Brittany. "In my opinion, Jason and I are the only couple qualified to win." Brittany fluffs her hair and glances at her opponent. "No offense, Katharine."

"None taken," said Katharine as she walks from the crowd to stand by Brittany on the stage. "Please vote for James and me. We don't want it to be a popularity contest this year. We need a change. We will appreciate all the votes that we receive."

"The dance will not be the same if we are not elected to be king and queen," said Brittany. "All votes are extremely important and deeply appreciated."

Jason found me in the crowd, and he looked directly at me. When our eyes met, I could tell by the look in his eyes that he was upset. That sorry look in his eyes was the one thing that connected me to the true Jason. I just don't understand why he is going to the ring dance with Brittany when he truly wanted to go with me. I am deeply heartbroken that he broke his promise to me. I guess, deep inside my heart, I knew this relationship was too good to be true.

I turned around so I wouldn't have to face Jason again. I was just too upset to look at him. My friends motioned me to follow them, and we walked away from the crowd to an empty space near the hallway.

"I can't believe he did this to me again. I was so excited about going to the dance with him, and plus, my mom has already bought that beautiful dress for me. I thought he was going to keep his promise by taking me to the dance, but I guess I was wrong."

I was so upset. My heart was pounding like a drum, and it felt like it was broken into a thousand pieces.

"You know what, guys? My mom was right. On the day we bought my dress, she had a feeling he was going to hurt me again. How could I be so stupid? I guess I should have listened to her. But . . . I am so in love with him that I forget about all of the bad things he has done to me. Well, he hasn't done all bad things; he has done good things, too."

"Why, I should punch him in the face for hurting you again," said Stanley.

"No, let's not do that."

"I am so sorry, Cynthia," said Melanie as she looked down at the floor.

"What are you going to do now?" Melody asked. "You already bought the dress. Are you still going to the dance?"

"I can't tell my mom that Jason is not taking me to the dance. That would truly break her heart. So, I am going to the dance by myself. It won't be the same as if I was going with him, but maybe it will be fun."

"Cynthia, you are not a junior," said Melanie. "I thought you could only go to the ring dance if you are accompanied by a junior."

"Yeah, you are right, Melanie. I was going to go with a junior, but he dumped me for another girl, so I am going to go anyway without him. Maybe something good will come of this."

"That sounds like a good idea," said Stanley as he winked at Melody and Melanie. "I think we are going to come to the dance, too. Crashing the Junior Ring dance sounds like fun. If you don't change your mind about going tomorrow, we will be there if you need us."

The day of the dance has finally arrived. I will probably be the only girl that will be dateless, "limo-less," and "bouquet-less," but I will be all right. You don't need to have all of those things to have fun at the dance. I still couldn't tell my mom that Jason wasn't going to take me to the dance. Maybe with time, I will tell her the truth. I just couldn't wait till this evening was over. I couldn't skip out of this event just because I had no date, and plus, I had a beautiful dress to wear. I couldn't let that go to waste.

I put on my dangling silver earrings and my pink heart necklace. I curled my hair, put on makeup, then tried on my dress. I looked in the mirror to see how everything looked together. I thought I looked so pretty. I put on the bracelet that Jason gave me and slowly walked down the stairs. I was finally having my princess moment but without my prince. I guess I was the girl who was still trying to find her prince. I know he is out there somewhere; I just have to find him.

"Oh, sweetheart," said my mother. "You look so beautiful. I can't wait to see Jason's face when he comes to pick you up."

"Mom, he said he would meet me at the dance," I told her. I hated lying to her, but I felt so ashamed that I got dumped right before the dance.

"Well . . . okay, honey," said my mom. "I will take you to the dance. But first, I want to take a picture of you in that beautiful dress."

I tried to keep a smile on my face since this was supposed to be one of the happiest nights of my life, which got ruined by Brittany, as usual.

My mom snapped another picture and showed both of them to my father.

"I can't wait to get these off my camera." My mom clicked the forward and backward arrows on her camera, trying to decide which picture of me was her favorite. She stood next to me and smiled while she showed me her camera screen. "I want to frame this one, so you can remember this special day."

My dad came behind us to glance at the picture. "Oh, that one is a beautiful picture of our Cynthia. I will have this framed and on the wall before you come home. I think I will place it right next to your brother's and sister's ring dance photos."

To them, it might have been a special day, but to me, it wasn't.

I arrived at the dance as the other princesses were getting out of their limousines. I heard the music blasting outside of the school. The next thing I noticed was the beautiful angel water fountain. The water fountain was sparkling more tonight than it does in the morning. I sat by the fountain in my pretty dress as I glanced down at the cold blue water. I could see my reflection as clear as I do in my mirror. I glided my hand through the cold but not icy water. As I watched the water follow my hand, the water began to make a small wave. Suddenly, my hand became extremely cold, so I took it immediately out of the water. I held my hand for a few minutes until it became warm again. I stood up and grabbed the side of my dress, and then I decided that I was ready to go inside the dance.

The music was blasting so hard that the hallway's walls were shaking. The dance room was filled with sparkly decorations, balloons, and blue confetti scattered all over the gymnasium floor. After I took a peek inside the gym, I walked down the hall and went inside the ladies' room to freshen up a bit. The bathroom was crowded. I guess every girl in the school had the same idea.

As I stood waiting for a mirror, I heard one of the girls speaking. "I can't believe how beautiful you look, Brittany."

Ugh, Brittany would be in the ladies' room at the same time as me.

"Thanks, girl," Brittany sighed. "Yeah, I am the most beautiful girl in here." She shook her hair, and her eyes looked off to the side. She rested her front teeth on her bottom lip as if she were a little hesitant to speak, and then her eyes brightened up. "No offense to the other girls in here."

"None taken," said a few girls who were brushing their hair at the vanity table.

Boy, does Brittany think she is hot stuff. I looked down at my dress, and then I looked in the mirror. I think I look as pretty as she does. On the other side of Brittany, I noticed there was an available seat at the vanity table, so I hurried and sat down in that spot before anyone else did.

Mandy turned around from fixing Brittany's hair and said, "You look really pretty tonight, Cynthia." Then she looked back at Brittany, who apparently was having a fit because her best friend was talking to me.

"I was just complimenting her dress, that's all," said Mandy.

"Oh my gosh," said Crystal. "I so agree. Cynthia does look beautiful in that dress."

"Ugh," Brittany said while rolling her eyes. "Girls, I am definitely ready to make my grand entrance now." Her two best friends and a few other girls in the bathroom were excited that Brittany was ready to enter the ballroom. Brittany stood up from her chair. "Jason," she said as she looked at me to make sure I was listening. "My boyfriend . . . is going to think I am absolutely gorgeous in this purple gown."

I was so glad that I was going to miss her grand entrance. It was nice that I received compliments from Mandy and Crystal, but it really made Brittany furious. But as things go with Brittany, she always redirects the focus right back to her. I am glad that she left the room so I can get a little peace. She is never going to let go of the memory of the first moment that I saw Jason. It is a little funny, by the way, that she is so paranoid about it, but I still can't believe that she still thinks that I am actually going to steal Jason away from her. It seems ridiculous. The way things are going with Jason and me, it just seems impossible for us to be together. But I don't want to worry about that right now. I am at a dance, and I want to try to have fun as long as I am here.

I reapplied my lipstick and moved my hair around a bit until I was pleased with the way it looked. Now, I was ready to make my grand entrance alone, but I was okay with that. As soon as I got to the gymnasium door, Brittany still hadn't walked into the dance yet. I guess she was waiting for me. Go figure. As I stood there, I noticed Jason standing in the middle of the ballroom. He looked really handsome in his white shirt and black tuxedo. Why did I have to see him? All of my feelings were coming back to me.

Jason walked across the dance floor toward Brittany. As he was reaching out his arm to hold Brittany's hand, he looked at me. Our eyes touched for one moment, but then, the romantic moment faded as he walked Brittany to the center of the dance floor.

I thought that was really sweet of him. Jason was being such a gentleman.

Stanley, who was early to the dance, came to me and said, "You look really beautiful, Cynthia." I guess I didn't have to make my grand entrance alone, after all. He smiled and grabbed my hand as we walked over to where Melody and Melanie were hanging out.

"Thanks, Stanley," I said as he twirled me around to show off my dress.

"Girl, you look so pretty," said Melody. "I wish I could pull off a dress as elegant as that, but you know how I am with girly clothes. This is probably the last time you will see me in a dress." We all laughed. "But anyway, I am so glad that you could make it."

"You sure do look pretty," said Melanie.

"We weren't sure if you were coming or not, but we are so glad you did," said Stanley.

"Guys, you know I couldn't let this beautiful dress go to waste. Just because I had a bad day yesterday doesn't mean I can't come to the dance today."

I smiled and gave all three of them a hug. The first outfit I noticed was Melanie's. Melanie was wearing a light blue dress with white heels. I thought she looked really pretty, and her white heels made her outfit pop. Melody was wearing a little black dress with silver shoes. I know Melody doesn't like dressing up, but I thought she looked really nice. But if I told her that to her face, I know she would deny it. And last but not least, Stanley was looking sharp. He had a few strands of hair out of place, but I like that look on him. His tuxedo was nicely pressed, and his black shoes were extra shiny.

Out of the blue, Melody cocked her nose up and said, "The snooty queen has arrived at the ball."

We all knew who she was talking about, and then we all laughed so hard that we almost fell on the floor.

A brown-haired lady wearing a shimmering blue dress came up to the front of the gymnasium. "Wow! Everyone looks great. My name is Brooke. I hope everyone is having a great time tonight. We will announce the king and queen in just a few minutes. Let's get this party started!" She raised her glass in the air, and then she took a sip.

All of the students raised their glasses and screamed, "Yeah!"

Melody, Melanie, Stanley, and I all began to dance when the music came back on. Stanley would dance with each of us, twirling one girl to the next. I bet Stanley enjoyed having three dates to the dance—lucky guy. Dancing with Stanley was so much fun. I didn't think the ring dance would be this awesome.

"This ring dance is so much fun!" Stanley yelled. "I am so glad that we all decided to crash this thingy!"

"So are we!" Melody and Melanie yelled over the music.

"Me too!" I yelled, even though I was invited but dumped right before the dance.

Twenty minutes went by, and Brooke came back to the front. "This is the moment you all have been waiting for. We have totaled all of your votes, and we are ready to announce the ring dance king and queen."

Everyone stood and waited as she opened her envelope. I already knew who they were going to pick anyway, but it was still exciting to watch. Although, it could change. Someone new may win for the title of king and queen, but I doubt it. However, it could happen, but in this school, that's rare. But it's a nice thought, though.

Brooke read the slip of paper and announced that Jason was the king. Jason walked up to the front, and Brooke placed a crown on his head. Jason stood there waiting as Brooke opened the second envelope naming the ring dance queen.

He looked so handsome standing there. Jason saw that I was looking at him, and he smiled at me. Quickly, I turned my head around, trying to pretend that I didn't see him smiling at me. I've been having trouble looking at Jason after all I have been through with him. When I look into his eyes, I fall back in love with him. I am trying to resist looking at him, which is really hard for me to do, but I am trying to protect myself from another heartbreak.

Instead of thinking about my broken heart from losing Jason, I focused my attention on the queen announcement. It was the only coping technique available to me at the moment. Brooke took a little piece of paper out of a small envelope and revealed the queen.

"Brittany Woods is the queen. This is her third win. Congratulations!" Brooke gave Brittany a hug, and then she placed a glittering crown on her head. To me, I thought Brittany had won a beauty pageant by the way Brooke congratulated her.

I was hoping Katharine would be queen instead of Brittany. I looked around the room for her since I knew how much she wanted to win. I finally found her. She was standing near the back wall in shock. I just felt so bad for Katharine. She deserved to win, not Brittany.

As I looked into Katharine's eyes, I began to see tears falling down her cheeks. She just couldn't hold in her tears any longer. She ran out of the gymnasium into the hall, and I suppose she went to the ladies' room. Well, usually, in this school, when a girl wants to be alone, they always go to the ladies' room. So, I just figured that's where she went.

"Now," said Brooke. "The king and queen will dance their first dance."

Jason grabbed Brittany's hand and danced with her while everyone watched. After Jason and Brittany danced for a few minutes alone, the rest of the students began to come forward to dance.

I couldn't believe how everything looked so beautiful. I stood there watching everyone, and suddenly I started to daydream of Jason and me dancing. He was dressed like a prince, and I was dressed like a princess. He bowed down to me, and I curtseyed to him. And then he grabbed and kissed my hand, and we waltzed around the ballroom. It was only a short daydream, but it felt so romantic and magical. I woke up from my daydream and noticed that Brittany and Jason stopped dancing. Jason grabbed Brittany's hand and walked her out into the hallway. No one knew that they quit dancing. I think I was the only one that really noticed that they were gone. I wasn't really worried about it, so I just continued to dance with Melody, Melanie, and Stanley. After three of my favorite songs played, I stopped dancing, as a worry came to my mind as Jason and Brittany had not returned to the dance.

"I think something is wrong," I said in a concerned voice. "Jason and Brittany have not come back yet."

"Why are you so worried about them?" Melody asked. "Just have fun and try to enjoy the night."

"Okay, I will." I know I told a mini lie, but I just can't have fun when Brittany isn't around. She could be up to something, and that makes me nervous. Maybe she has more tricks up her sleeve to make my life more miserable, as usual. Doing that is probably one of her goals in life. But at least when I can see her, I know that she's not up to something mysterious. I searched every corner and place around the room . . . still no Jason and Brittany in sight. I wasn't worried about Brittany so much, she is a tough girl, but the one person I was worried about was Jason. I have to go find them if it's the last thing I do.

I started to walk out, and Stanley grabbed my arm. "Where are you going?"

"I need some air. I want to walk around a bit."

Stanley nodded and continued dancing.

I walked down the hall quietly to see if I could hear or see anybody. So far, I heard no one. But as I walked closer to the school's main entrance, I heard two people yelling.

"Of all the nights, Jason, you want to talk," yelled the girl.

"We need to talk about this fake dating thing," said Jason. "I don't want to do this anymore."

"Well, you should have said something before," said the girl in an angry manner.

I was near the main entrance, and I could see Jason and Brittany fighting by the fountain. Brittany was furious with Jason, kind of like the way she was with me in the bathroom, but the situation is worse now. I could tell that by her angry expression and her placement of her hands on her hips. While Jason, on the other hand, was upset but in a calm-like manner. Ryan was already standing by the door listening to them fight when I got here. He seemed really entertained by it all.

At that moment, Jason continued, "I tried to, but you wouldn't listen to me." Brittany looked like she was about to say something, but Jason interrupted her. "I want to be myself . . . not this guy you apparently like."

"Jason, why are you doing this to me?" Brittany asked. "Don't you love me anymore?"

"Actually, I don't love you," said Jason. "I love someone else." He turned his head to the side, and he noticed that I was by the doorway watching. Our eyes connected romantically. It was like we were the only ones here.

"Why you?" Brittany yelled. She raised her arm and swung her hand close to Jason's face.

"Jason, watch out," I yelled to get his attention.

Immediately, Jason focused his attention from me to Brittany in just a quick second. He grabbed her wrist gently to prevent her from slapping him, and when Brittany struggled to get her hand loose from Jason's grasp, she lost her balance and fell directly into the fountain.

Ryan was so excited by what had happened that he ran down the hall to announce the news. Ryan reached the gym and shouted, "The ring dance queen is soaked. Brittany lost her balance and fell directly into the fountain."

Everyone was shocked and yelling loudly at one another, retelling the great news.

Katharine came out of the bathroom, wiping her face. She was stunned by the multitude of people in the hallway. "What's going on? Why is everyone so noisy?"

Ryan came out from the crowd. "Brittany and Jason got into a fight. Jason was trying to prevent Brittany from slapping him, so he grabbed her hand. Brittany was trying to release her hand from Jason's grasp, and she lost her balance and fell right into the fountain."

"What?" Katharine said in shock. "I have got to see this."

A mass of people, including Ryan and Katharine, ran down the hall to see the drama queen drenched in water.

"Why, you jerk!" Brittany screamed. "Look at my dress. You ruined it. This is supposed to be the most magical day of my life, and you ruined it. This is all your fault, Jason."

Jason looked from me to Brittany. He seemed unsure about what to do. He walked over to Brittany, and he placed out his hand to help her up. "I am sure you will have other days that are more magical than this one. Let me help you up."

"No! Leave me alone, Jason. You have done enough." Brittany splashed her hands in the water, and everyone started to laugh at her. Brittany looked around at the large number of people surrounding her. "This is not funny, guys. This is so humiliating." A few seconds later, Brittany's skirt bubbled up. When everyone saw that, they started to laugh even harder. Brittany pushed her skirt down and rested her head on her hands while trying to keep her skirt from popping up. Brittany sat there, and her eyes began to weep while hidden underneath the covering of her hands.

Jason ran to me. "Cynthia, you are the one that I love. I should have taken you to the dance as I promised. Will you please forgive me?"

I stood there and started to think. At that moment, I suddenly noticed that Jason's face was sweating while he stood there anxiously waiting for my answer. When the time was right, I smiled and said, "You know I will."

I am glad that Jason finally stood up to Brittany. He is finally comfortable with being himself. It took him a while, but I am glad he is now the man I love. You shouldn't be afraid to be yourself. People will like you for who you are, and you don't have to be untrue to yourself to get them to like you. Your true friends will stick by you, no matter what.

Jason and I walked back inside to an empty ballroom.

"May I have this dance?" Jason bent forward slightly as he reached out his hand to grab mine.

"Of course," I said with a smile as I touched his hand.

We danced around the room, and it was so romantic and magical. This dance turned out to be the most special day of my life. The daydream of dancing with Jason has finally come true. I have found my prince, and I am the happiest girl in the world. I hope this night never ends.

ABOUT THE AUTHOR

Becky Archibald started to love to read and write at a young age. She loves animals and even had a cat that lived for twenty-one years. She always had an idea of writing a book about this cat and how she saw her as popular.

Ever since Becky began to write this story about this group of friends and the troubles they face, she hasn't looked back. She wants this book to inspire young people to not be afraid to be themselves and to seek help if they are being bullied.

In her spare time, Becky likes to watch videos on her phone. She also like to read fashion magazines and books about fairy tales. She currently lives in Virginia with her cat Simon.